W9-ABQ-907

FLIGHT
of the
MOTH-KIN

FLIGHT
of the
MOTH-KIN

Kathy Kennedy Tapp

illustrated by Michele Chessare

Margaret K. McElderry Books
NEW YORK

Margaret K. McElderry Books
Macmillan Publishing Company
866 Third Avenue
New York, NY 10022
Collier Macmillan Canada, Inc.

Composition by V & M Graphics Inc.
New York, New York
Printed and bound by Fairfield Graphics
Fairfield, Pennsylvania

First Edition

10   9   8   7   6   5   4   3   2   1

Library of Congress Cataloging-in-Publication Data

Tapp, Kathy Kennedy.
Flight of the moth-kin.

Summary: Having escaped the giants' glass bottle prison,
tiny Moth-kins brave the dangers of what seems to be a human
playground as they attempt to return to their colony by the river
with the aid of their newly developed wings.
[1. Fantasy.   2. Size—Fiction]
I. Chessare, Michele, ill.   II. Title.
PZ7.T1646F1   1987   [Fic]   87-3940
ISBN 0-689-50401-2

*Dedicated with love
to the memory of my mother,
my father,
my sister Patricia*

Contents

"In the days of Pan and Fern and Kane and the children, Crick, Lissa, and Ripple, there came a great invasion of giants. And the giants destroyed their homes and captured them and put them in a silent forest. They put a wall around the forest. When the prisoners schemed to get out, the giants put their poison scent into the forest. And they raked the ground with their claw.

"But the prisoners escaped. They turned the evil claw of the giants against them. They braved great dangers and traveled to a far-distant land. And all this they did before the coming of the magic."

The story of the Moth-Kins
as told by Lissa at the First
Gathering in the New Land.

The New Land

The forest was huge. The trees seemed to touch the sky itself. Great six-legged insect-beasts stalked the grasses. Enormous birds swooped overhead.

Ripple took a deep breath, then another, as she pushed through the high grasses. Her heart thumped wildly. Her whole body tingled with the danger, the excitement.

"We're pioneers," she whispered to Crick and Lissa. "Pioneers in a new land!"

"Careful . . . be careful!" Mother's voice was a faint echo in the distance.

Ripple glanced back. Mother and Uncle Kane and Pan were standing at the edge of camp; three small figures almost lost in the vast greenness of the forest. It was too far away to see their faces clearly, but Ripple could picture the worried look on Mother's face. Uncle's hand was raised. Was it a wave? Or was he still lecturing—"They are too young to go off exploring by themselves!"

"Hurry!" Lissa said. "Before they change their minds and call us back."

Ripple lifted her own hand in a quick wave and hurried after Crick and Lissa. "Lucky for us Pan talked Uncle and Mother into letting us go," she said.

"Well, we *are* old enough to hike alone. And brave enough—didn't we just escape from the giants' bottle prison?" Crick bragged. "And we'll never learn anything about this land—or find a new home—by sitting around in that shelter." He parted the grasses. "Come on!"

They pushed deeper into the forest, moving cautiously, checking at each step for insect-beasts: dragon-wings, web-spinners, antennae-creatures, enemies that could crush them in powerful jaws or kill them with great stingers or pincers. Crick cut slashes in the bark of the low branches along the way to mark their trail.

"We're scouts," Ripple whispered to the others. "Brave scouts exploring new territory. We'll be able to tell them all about this forest when we go back." All her life Ripple had wanted to be a scout. Her father had been one—until he failed to return from a mission. And now, here she was on a great adventure in a new land. And what a forest!

Crick waved his newly made spear stick in the

air. "A little more practice with this, and I'll be killing those insect-beasts single-handed," he boasted.

"Me too!" Ripple waved her own stick.

Lissa pushed her long, dark hair off her face and stared up at the sky. "Maybe we should head back," she said. "They didn't want us to stay too long this first time."

"That's the way back." Crick pointed with his spear. He raced back, then bent over, checking the branches of a bush.

"I made a slash in this one. . . ." He parted the leaves to study the bush closer, frowning. "I can't find the mark."

"What?" Ripple ran toward him, searching the branches. "If you made it, it's got to be there."

"Are you sure it was this bush?" Lissa asked, searching too.

"I . . . I. . . ." For once, proud, confident Crick didn't sound too sure. He looked around. "I thought it was this one. . . ." His voice trailed off.

Ripple felt her stomach plunging like a stone down to her toes. "But . . . but . . . ." She couldn't quite get the words out. She looked around frantically. "Maybe it was that bush."

They ran toward it, searching the trunk, the branches. There was no slash on it, either.

Ripple gazed at the great forest spreading out around them in all directions. Weeds, bushes, plants, trees, everywhere. Suddenly, they all looked the same.

"We didn't hike too far from the shelter," she said, trying to sound calm. "We can find our way back, even without the trail."

This hike was important. They *had* to find their way back quickly, without trouble. This hike was a test, to prove to the adults that the three of them were old enough to be scouts. Especially to Uncle. Ripple could still hear his parting words:

"Young ones aren't skilled enough in camouflage!" Uncle had cried over and over, frowning under his bushy white eyebrows. "There are too many dangers in the wild! They haven't enough experience!"

But Pan had trusted them. He'd convinced Mother and Uncle that they could manage. "It'll be good training for them," he'd said.

And now here they were—lost, the very first time out.

"I think it's . . . that way," Crick said uncertainly. He strode ahead. "Ye . . . es, this must be right."

They pushed on. The forest no longer seemed an exciting new wilderness to explore. The bushes and weeds closed around them menacingly. Ripple grasped her spear tightly, trying to fight back the feeling of panic.

"We've been in danger lots of times," she said, eyeing the weeds fearfully for legs, stingers, death-webs. "We've always made it through. We'll get back."

"The pioneers in the old times probably got lost sometimes, too," Lissa added.

"Right," Ripple said stoutly. "And they made it through. We will, too." She and Lissa both loved the old legends that Uncle Kane told of the heroes of their people, the Moth-Kin.

Their people had a great history. No matter that they were so small in a world full of huge things: huge plants, huge insects, and worst of all—huge giants with arms and legs and great stomping feet. Ripple shuddered. She didn't want to think about giants.

Her people were strong. They were smart. They were brave. And their greatest strength of all would come soon: the magic. The magic of wings came to them during the warm season each year.

Just thinking about the wings made her feel better. She had watched it happen to others in her old colony each year. And now this year she was old enough finally for the magic to come to her, too. So were Crick and Lissa.

"If we had our wings," she whispered, "we could find our way back easily."

"But we don't," Crick said.

"Maybe we should call—" Lissa began.

"And do you know what would happen, dreamhead?" Crick snapped at his sister. "All the enemy creatures in this whole forest would know exactly where we are. Diy!"

"Diy" was Crick's special word. It could mean anything from happiness to surprise to anger. Right now it meant fear, the same fear growing in Ripple—the fear that they might not find their way back to the shelter-camp.

They hiked farther. With each step Ripple became more convinced that they were going the wrong way. There was no sign of a trail left by their trampling feet, no gashes that should have been there to guide them back, no sign of the camp, where Mother, Pan, and Uncle were no doubt starting to worry.

Something else was wrong. Ripple could hear a noise, a heavy stomping sound different from the insect buzzes and bird chirps. It was getting louder, closer.

"Do you hear that noise?" she whispered. "It's practically shaking the ground."

"Maybe we'd better turn back." Crick moved in a half-crouch. "There's something big out there." He took a few more cautious steps, then pushed back the weeds.

"What—"

The three of them stared in shock.

The forest had ended, suddenly, abruptly. They stood facing a sea of tall, waving grass that seemed to stretch ahead forever. Then Ripple saw something else—towering above the grasses—that made her dive for the ground, bringing Lissa down with her.

"Giants." It was barely a whisper. She stared through the grasses in horror. There was no mistaking those enormous legs that rose like trees toward the sky. Somewhere above the legs were arms, heads, faces. Somewhere below them were horrible stomping feet.

She started shaking. Those feet—she'd run from them before—almost got crushed by them before.

"Are the giants looking for us? Did they follow us here?"

"I thought we escaped the giants!" Crick hissed, pressing low, his fist tight on his spear. "I thought we didn't have to worry about them in this land."

"The noise—" Lissa murmured, white-faced. "It was them, stomping the ground."

Ripple nodded numbly. What kind of a place

was this, anyway? A colony of giants? The forest was not so huge, after all. It had led them to a land of giants and grass.

"We . . . have . . . to . . . get . . . away." Ripple started backing up, her eyes still glued in

terror to the awful sight of those legs. "Come on."
She could hardly talk. Her mouth, her whole body
felt frozen. She crawled backwards, slowly, as if
in a daze. "They'll find us, stomp on us—"

"Ripple, look out!" Crick yelled.

Ripple whirled around, too late. The insect-
beast was but a step away, standing there on
great stick legs, with round bulbous eyes fixed
on her and great jaws opening.

In that frozen second of terror she saw something else—no, some*one*—moving near a
thornbush up ahead. Someone hunched over, with
long, tangled gray hair.

A pain like fire sliced at Ripple's left leg.
Then everything went black.

II

The Humpbacked Woman

"Ripple—Ripple."

Lissa's voice. She sounded very far away.

Ripple opened her eyes. Lissa's and Crick's faces blurred above her.

"What—happened?" she whispered. She felt hot. Her leg hurt.

"The insect-beast bit you," Crick said.

Lissa leaned over and pushed back Ripple's tangled hair. "Oh, Ripple, I'm so glad you woke up! Your leg looked awful. Old Ivy helped us carry you here."

"Old Ivy?" Ripple looked around, confused. She rubbed her eyes. "Who's that?"

"She lives here," Lissa whispered. "She put those leaves on your leg for medicine. She's out getting more leaves right now."

"She gave us these tunics to help us hide better in the grasses."

Ripple sat up, peering closer at her two friends. Her head was clearer now; for the first time she noticed the strange tunics they were both wearing. They were woven in many shades of green, with brown patches throughout. It made them look strangely wild: Lissa, with her long, dark hair flowing about her face, and Crick, with a woven headband circling his forehead.

"But—where are we?" Ripple felt more and more confused. She stared around the dim room, at the shiny, gray, tunnel-like walls and the small, round doorway. When she reached out a hand to touch the shiny wall, it made a dull clinking sound. She pulled back. "What *is* this place? I never saw a shelter like this!"

"Old Ivy's tunnel-shelter." Lissa leaned closer, lowering her voice. "She lives here all alone."

"I've seen this kind of can-thing before," Crick added. "In the garden, where Lissa and Pan and I used to live. It had brown, sweet, watery stuff inside. I tasted it. Pan told us giants *drink* from tunnel-cans like this."

"Pan—" Ripple cut in eagerly, "Mother, Uncle . . . did you . . . ?"

Lissa shook her head. "I suppose they're out looking for us, but we haven't heard them. It's hard to hear anything, with the giants' noise so loud all the time."

"But we have to find them!" Ripple tried to stand. The world started to spin. She lay back, dizzily. "Later," she whispered. "I'll be strong enough in a little while. We've got to . . . find them."

Ripple dreamed. Lots of dreams. And every dream was about the river. The wonderful splashing river where she had lived all her life until the trouble started with the giants. In her dreams she was playing with the other children of the colony, running along the riverbank. Mother was there. And Uncle Kane. Everyone was laughing, playing, splashing.

She opened her eyes. The dream had been so real. She half-expected to see water and fishing nets and—

Instead, she was alone in the dim shelter-can. Shiny, gray walls stared at her. A basket of seeds lay beside her. The sight made her stomach growl with hunger. She stuffed in a mouthful, then washed them down with water from a seed pod container.

Where were Crick and Lissa? The pain in her leg was much better. And the food made her feel stronger. She moved slowly toward the round doorway, limping a little, and stared out.

There were branches everywhere. Dark, twisted branches with long thorns reaching down on all sides. Except for a small clearing by the doorway, branches completely surrounded the tunnel-can in a great thorn web.

Ripple looked around in amazement. Even giants wouldn't be able to penetrate such a defense. She took a few slow steps forward, then stopped.

At the far edge of the clearing, almost hidden by the overhanging thorn branches, was the old woman. She had gray, tangled hair, a brown, leathery face, and she was wearing a long green-brown cape that covered her from shoulders to feet—but it did not hide the hump on her back.

She was bent over, sprinkling something on the dirt. And—Ripple's eyes widened—she was talking out loud.

"Don't try to fool Old Ivy, now. I know you like these seeds, ugly beasts. Go on. Take them."

Ripple looked around, bewildered. Who was the old woman talking to?

Then, as Ripple watched in horror, a creeper suddenly moved from a small dirt hill and started toward the seeds. It picked one up in its mouth and moved away quickly on its stick-like legs. Another creeper followed, and another, and another; a great marching line to the seeds. They were smallish creepers. But even so, Ripple took a step backward. Creepers BIT! Didn't the old woman know that? Surely she would move away, too?

But she just stood there calmly watching, as the creepers moved right by her without even stopping.

"All right, all right, that's enough," she said finally. Her voice was bossy, scolding, not in the least afraid. "Be off with you, greedy beasts." Then she turned and saw Ripple.

"Well, so you're up," Old Ivy said in almost the same tone she had used on the creepers. She studied Ripple for a moment. "How are you feeling?"

Ripple swallowed. "Those . . . creepers," she faltered. Her voice sounded embarrassingly squeaky. "How . . . ?"

"They're used to the smell of me." The old woman dismissed them with a wave of her hand. "They're just stupid creatures, really."

Ripple took another step back. She wanted to run away, as far as she could from this crazy humpbacked woman who talked to creepers.

"Where are Crick and Lissa?" Her voice wobbled.

"They've gone off."

"*What!*" Ripple's legs suddenly felt like soggy vines. "They wouldn't! They wouldn't leave me!"

"Poppy-rot," Old Ivy said sharply. "They

haven't left you at all. They'll be back. And soon." She held out the basket of seeds. "Here, eat," she commanded. "Food is what you need."

Ripple shook her head, pushing away the basket that had fed creepers. "No. I don't want it."

Old Ivy raised her eyebrows. "You're a stubborn one, aren't you?" Then her expression changed. "What did I tell you? Here comes one of your friends now."

At the same moment Ripple heard a rustling noise at the edge of the thorn branches. Then Lissa's voice, high, excited: "Ripple, look!"

Ripple spun around.

"L—lissa," she stammered, "you . . . you. . . ."

Lissa's face was one big, glorious smile. She ran toward Ripple. "It happened! Look! Look at me, Ripple!"

Ripple stared at the clear membranes arching from Lissa's back. They were shiny-wet with newness, and criss-crossed with fine veins. Wings. Real wings.

The magic had come to Lissa.

"What does it feel like? How long did it take? What *happens*? Did Crick get them too?"

"I don't know. It's like . . . being asleep. I don't know how to describe it. Or where Crick is." Lissa shook her head helplessly. Then she reached out and squeezed Ripple's hand. "It'll come to you next. Anytime now."

Lissa looked like a princess, standing so straight and proud, with the magic wings glowing like sunshine. She took a few steps, then rose slowly into a low glide, moving gracefully through a small gap in the thorn-branch wall.

"I'll look for him," she called back.

Ripple clenched her fists, watching.

Wings! She wanted them so badly! She walked across the clearing, head high, then pushed through the thorn branches. She blinked as bright sunlight hit her eyes. Sunlight and green; the green of high waving grass all around her.

Old Ivy's thornbush stood just outside the giants' grassland, then. But the place was quiet now. No hideous stomping feet, no terrifying rumbles, no enormous legs.

But there were other things rising from the grasses that she hadn't noticed before. Now, standing on a slight hill, she could see contraptions as tall as trees, glinting in the sun.

They were evil giants' things. Ripple knew it instinctively. The whole grassland was evil.

"Oh, Lissa, let's get away from here." She grabbed her friend's arm, as Lissa landed beside her. "As soon as Crick is back. We have to look for the others. That old woman—she's crazy! She talks to creepers! Can you believe it? I heard her. She even feeds them!"

Lissa looked troubled. "I think she's been alone a long time, with no one to talk to *but* creepers." She dropped her voice. "I wonder who she is. How she got here. Do you think she's one of our kind—a Moth-Kin?"

"Her back is all humped. She couldn't ever have wings," Ripple pointed out. "So how could she be one of us?"

"Well, then, who *is* she?"

"I don't know. And anyway, it's the others we have to find. Pan and Mother and Uncle Kane." Just saying the names made a burning lump form in Ripple's throat. "They're in the forest some-where. We have to find them! And Crick, too."

Lissa bit her lip, looking back at the thornbush, then toward the forest. "Well, my wings should help us—"

"And my leg's better. We could—" Ripple broke off at a sudden sound. "Did you hear some-thing?"

"What?"

"There it is again. Hear it?" The noise came faintly over the buzzing of the grass creatures. Then again, louder. It was a voice.

"Crick! That's my brother's voice!" Lissa

grabbed Ripple's hand so hard it hurt. "He's in trouble!"

Her wings spread, and she was gone.

III

The Mud Rescue

Ripple thrashed through the grasses.

"Crick!" she yelled frantically. "Crick, where are you?" She limped faster, ignoring the ache in her leg. "Crick! Lissa!"

"What in the name of all the heroes are you trying to do? Let every enemy creature in the whole forest know where you are?" A hand caught her arm. "Shh!" Old Ivy hissed fiercely. Her grip was firm, hard.

Ripple struggled to break free. "Crick's in trouble!"

"And so will you be if you don't quiet down! Haven't you learned your lesson yet?" the old woman demanded sternly.

They glared at each other. Ripple shook free angrily.

"Now, stay with me and we will find him,"

Old Ivy ordered.

There was no time for the sharp reply forming on Ripple's tongue. The next moment Old Ivy melted into the grasses.

"Come. This way." Her movements and the colors of her cape blended with the grasses so well, it was hard to keep her in sight.

Ripple hurried after her, half-hopping. Her leg throbbed. Worry and fear raced through her.

"Here! Over here!" Lissa's voice called out. Ripple looked around frantically.

"Where are you!" she yelled.

Then she saw Lissa standing at the top of a small hill, waving her arms. "Up here!" A huge, gleaming white tower rose behind her, reaching up toward the sky.

"The bird tower," said Old Ivy. "It's a dangerous place."

Ripple stumbled up the hill, toward the gleaming tower. Then she stopped so fast she fell.

There was a stout figure just ahead. A wonderfully familiar stout figure with long matted beard and torn tunic, and thick yellowed wings.

"*Uncle!*" she yelled, scrambling to her feet.

He spun around—and dropped the armload of weeds he was carrying.

"Dear Nimrod," he whispered. His face went as white as his beard. "Ripple—"

Ripple was afraid the old man was going to fall over, he looked so shaken. She ran to him, flinging her arms around him in a tight hug.

"Uncle, it's *you*. It's *you*. I found you!"

"We searched and searched for you children." Uncle Kane's usually powerful voice sounded hoarse. "We thought we'd never see you again. Thank the Mighty One *you're* safe. . . ." Then he shook his head as if to clear it. "But there's no time for talk. They're caught in the mud. We need a rope, to get them out."

"What!" Ripple stared at him in horror. "Who! Where!"

"We heard Crick yelling for help. Your mother tried to pull him out. Now she's caught too," Uncle said, grabbing weeds, pushing up the hill, huffing and panting. "Hurry, girl! Get some weeds!"

But Ripple hardly heard his last words; she was already halfway up the hill, tripping over weed stubble, holes and pebbles. Her leg hurt, her head buzzed. Crick and Mother—caught in treacherous sucking mud—it was like a bad dream.

"Ripple, up here! Hurry!" There was Lissa again, waving her arms wildly. And she was not alone. Pan stood beside her, knotting weeds. Tall, strong Pan with tunic ripped, face mud-spattered, and wings, strong and hard, arching from his back. A wonderful feeling of relief washed through Ripple, seeing him. Pan could take care of any problem. There was no better person in an emergency. He could get them out of mud. Pan could do just about anything.

She ran toward them. Then she saw the mud, on the other side of the hill. The gleaming white tower rose out of the huge mudhole. And in the middle of the oozing mud were two small figures—

"Mother!" Ripple screamed. "Crick!" She started toward them.

Hands grasped her shoulders. She whirled to find herself looking into Pan's piercing blue eyes.

"Stay away from the mud." His fingers gripped her shoulders tightly. "We'll get them out. We need weeds, fast—"

"Those flimsy weeds won't do." Suddenly Old Ivy stood beside them, her arms full of bristly thick fibers. No words of introduction. She was just suddenly there. "Here, you need this kind." She tossed a handful to Pan, then started knotting some herself with quick, sure fingers.

Uncle Kane came into sight, huffing, red-faced, his beard matted with the weeds he carried. "Here's more!" he panted. "Hurry, man, we're losing time!"

Pan knotted fast and furiously, adding his section to Ivy's. "Lissa," he said, his voice sharp, urgent. "Fly this end of the rope out to them. Don't let your body touch the muck. That's how Fern got caught, trying to pull Crick up." Then he turned to the others. "When Crick and Fern get hold of their end, we pull."

"Mud is nothing to fool around with," muttered Uncle. "Crick was probably trying some fool trick with his new wings. Young whippersnapper."

As Lissa flew out over the mud, Ripple braced herself between Pan and Uncle and grasped the rough fiber.

"Fool boy," Uncle muttered again. Then, looking at Ripple, "Such a day!" He looked dazed, in shock. "Too much for an old man!"

"Ready—one, two, three—*pull*!" Pan cried.

At first nothing happened.

"Don't break, rope," Lissa whispered, flying back to grab the rope.

"Pull. *Pull*!" Pan's eyes never left the two in the mud.

"We are pulling!" Uncle yelled back. "Cursed mud!" He sneezed, a great snorty sneeze that shook his stout body free of the rope. "There's alanine weed somewhere! It always starts me off!"

Ripple leaned so far back, she was afraid she'd fall right over. Her leg throbbed, her shoulders

ached, the rope weed burned her hands. Still she pulled. She could hear Pan's hard breathing, Uncle's grunts, Lissa's panting, Old Ivy's fierce murmur, "Al . . . most . . . got . . . it. . . ."

There was a cry from the mud.

"It's working! They're coming free!"

"Keep pulling!"

They grabbed, grunted, heaved, braced their feet, grabbed again, pulling hand over hand, dragging the two figures closer through the thick oozing muck.

"That's it—keep pulling." Pan breathed each word as he pulled. They were almost within reach.

Ripple could see the exhaustion and disbelief in her mother's face, as her eyes found Ripple.

"Mother!" Ripple half sobbed the word, reaching out to grab her mother's mud-covered arm. Pan took the other, while Lissa and Uncle and Old Ivy pulled Crick free. Sputtering and gasping, the two tumbled onto the bank.

Then mud enveloped Ripple. Muddy arms, muddy tunic, a wrenching, mud-soaking embrace. Mud mixed with tears and grass and weeds. Mother was crying, hugging her, hugging Pan, Crick, Lissa, saying things that Ripple couldn't hear or understand, through all the noise: voices interrupting, crying, everyone pressing in to become part of the mud hug.

"I was trying a spin glide," Crick said weakly. "I didn't know the mud would suck me in."

"By Nimrod, my heart will never be the same." Uncle sat down heavily. "Such a day!"

"We never would have made it without that extra rope." Pan looked over at Old Ivy.

The talking and hugging stopped. Mother and Uncle Kane stared at the old woman. She had put her cape on again, and drawn it tightly around her. Her hair was spread out in its usual tangle, and her wrinkled face was spattered with mud. Her hands were busy pulling at weed strands, one after another, as she stood proudly apart, watching them.

"Old Ivy, this is our group . . . " Lissa faltered. "Pan, Fern, Uncle Kane. . . ." As Lissa gestured toward each one, a funny feeling crept over Ripple. Her eyes had noticed already, but her brain hadn't paid attention during the emergency. But now, as her eyes went from one loved person to the next, she took in one important inescapable fact.

Pan, Mother, Uncle, Crick, Lissa all had wings.

IV

The Giants' Weapon

"Hurry. Away from that tower. It's not safe here." Old Ivy kept looking up, as if she expected to see an enemy swoop down from the sky any second. "Birds come to this white tower. They splash water. That is why there is so much mud." And without waiting to see if anyone was following, she started toward a nearby bush, melting instantly into the grasses.

"No rest for the weary." Uncle heaved a great sigh, pulling himself to his feet. He stared back at the gleaming white tower rising out of the mud and the grasses waving all around. "An *evil* place," he muttered darkly. "Birds, giants, great ugly contraptions. Evil, I tell you." He pushed irritably through the grasses, rubbing at the mud that had caked on his arms and face.

But Ripple only half heard his gloomy mutterings. She just kept looking at Mother, who was beautiful even under layers of mud, at Pan, with his sharp blue eyes and his beloved lantan weed dangling from his mouth and—his arm around Mother's shoulder. The sight made Ripple smile just a little. Mother and Pan. Mother and Pan. The names seemed to go together lately.

And, of course, poor old Uncle Kane, hobbling, complaining, cursing, but still keeping up with the rest of them, as always. His wings were thicker, less fine-veined, than the others'.

Wings. Her eyes went back to the wings each time. Crick's were shiny-thin with newness, like Lissa's. Mother's looked strong, like Pan's.

Ripple's hand reached back to touch the empty space between her shoulder blades. Longing rushed through her. When? When would the magic come to her? Why was it taking longer than with the others?

"There. We can rest under that bush." Old Ivy led them to a tall bush covered with small, round leaves.

"Ah, finally." Uncle sank to the ground with a grunt of relief. "This old body wasn't meant for such strenuous tasks."

Crick and Lissa launched into the story of their hike. Ripple hugged her knees to her chin and tried hard to keep her mind on the story, to keep her eyes away from the wondrous wings. "It'll come," she told herself fiercely. "It'll come. Magic comes to everything in its own time."

"—and then the insect-beast bit Ripple—"

"*What!*" Mother grasped Ripple by the shoulders, her eyes wide with horror. "One of those awful beasts! Those bites can be deadly!"

"I'm all right," Ripple protested. "Really." It was almost true. The dizzy, sick feeling was long since gone. And she was getting used to the dull throbbing. Soon that would probably disappear, too.

"Old Ivy put medicine leaves on the bite," Lissa said.

Mother turned to Old Ivy. "You saved Ripple's life." She opened her mouth to say more, but Uncle stood up just then, shaking his finger at Ripple, Crick, and Lissa.

"You are lucky to be alive to tell the tale! Such behavior was as reckless and foolhardy as Crick's somersaulting into the mud!"

"It wasn't a somersault! It was a spin-glide. I wanted to see what the white tower was."

"Spin-glide, somersault, no matter!" Uncle bellowed. "The three of you need to learn caution, if you are going to survive in this forest! One hike—just one little hike it was going to be. And look what's happened to you! Lost, bitten, almost drowned in mud! The pioneers of old never showed such foolhardiness!"

"Poppy-rot. Young ones never know better,"

Old Ivy said. "They always learn the hard way."

Uncle's mouth opened and shut again. "Well . . . well . . . " he sputtered. He adjusted his muddy tunic. "Well, be that as it may. . . . " Then his voice swelled to its full commanding tone: "They must learn the skills of survival!"

Ripple watched in complete and utter amazement. No one ever spoke to Uncle Kane that way. But Old Ivy was still sitting there calmly. The sky hadn't fallen on her yet. There were even little crinkles around the corners of her eyes, as if she were enjoying herself. Pan and Mother were exchanging little smiles, too.

Rumble stomp thud. The sound came from somewhere far across the grasslands. The sound of giants.

The next moment there was a whizzing noise overhead. Ripple looked up in time to see a huge red thing, like a gigantic river berry, hurtle through the branches overhead.

"*Down!*" Mother cried.

They all dove toward the center of the bush, as the huge round thing crashed down through the branches and slammed into the ground. Even then it did not stop, but incredibly, it bounced back off the ground, hit another branch, fell to the earth again, and rolled to a stop.

"Attack! Attack of the giants!" Uncle's voice

was a hoarse croak. "They're throwing weapons! They know we're here."

Pan jumped up. "Hurry—up into the bush," he ordered. "They'll be coming after that thing."

"After *us*, you mean!"

Ripple scrambled up into the branches, trying to keep her weight off her sore leg. Her heart thumped wildly. Her hair and tunic caught on the rough bark. Crick and Lissa were just above her.

"Higher!"

"Oomph, these old bones can't move that fast. May those giants be cursed with the bites of a thousand antennae-creatures!"

Rumble stomp thud. The ground shook. The whole bush trembled. Leaves whipped about wildly. Ripple clung to her branch.

And then her heart stopped.

An enormous hand was reaching in through the branches, right below her. She could see the five fingers like long, fleshy worm-snakes, with claws at the ends. She could see the hair on the giant's arm; she could hear the giant's heavy breathing . . . as those hideous fingers moved in closer, feeling the ground.

Uncle was right. The giants had discovered them. First they'd thrown their round red weapon; now they were coming in for the kill—or the capture.

Fear poured through Ripple's body in hot waves. The branch shook with the trembling of her body. Her palms were so sweaty she was sure she would lose her grip any second and fall right on that mountain of an arm. This was *it*.

The horrible fingers closed around the red object with a grip that squeezed it into puckers. Such cruel, hard strength. Ripple pressed against her branch desperately, trying to melt into the bark, to look invisible, to make no sound, not even to breathe.

Then the hand jerked back, taking the weapon with it.

The bush shook again. The ground rumbled with footfalls, and the giant was gone.

They'd been spared. For some mysterious reason the giant had not taken them this time. But the terror of the last few minutes had left Ripple feeling as limp as if the giant's hand had squeezed *her* in those fat finger snakes.

"Dear Nimrod," Mother said faintly. "Will this nightmare never end?"

"We are doomed," Uncle muttered from his hiding place behind a gnarled branch stub. "Surrounded by a colony of giants. They will follow us wherever we go. We cannot get away from them. They are everywhere."

"They *are* everywhere." Crick's voice spoke

from the other side of a leaf clump, full of wonder and fear. "Diy—they're all over the grassland. Just look at them!"

Ripple's arms and legs were still shaky. She crawled toward Crick slowly, clutching the bark ridges for support.

"Over here." Crick was crouched at the tip of the branch. He motioned her toward him. "Just *look* at all of them," he whispered.

Ripple stared. From the height of the branch she could see out over the grassland; she could really see the huge contraptions rising out of the grasses and the great bodies of the giants *on* the contraptions.

Her hand went to her mouth. "What are they doing?" she whispered.

The giants were performing strange ceremonies on their contraptions.

One contraption was a great long plank. There was a giant sitting at each end of the plank. One giant went up, and the other giant went down. Up and down. Up and down. Amazing.

Near the plank was an enormous round platform. Lots of ugly giants were sitting on it. Ripple's eyes bugged out in wonder, watching the round thing spin around and around, whirling the giants faster and faster. Incredible.

In another part of the grassland, giants were

sitting on seat-things which hung from long ropes. They were gliding back and forth, back and forth. And just beyond that, other giants seemed to be climbing up a great shiny hill, then sliding down it. Unbelievable.

The giants were not only huge and lumbering. They were also crazy.

"Mighty Moth-Kin," Crick breathed. "Have you ever heard of such a thing?"

"But why are they doing it?" Lissa spoke in a low, frightened whisper. She turned to the adults who crouched behind them, watching the unbelievable scene. "What does it *mean?*"

No one answered. Even Pan, who knew more than anyone about the giants, just shook his head.

"And we thought we escaped them," Mother murmured. "We were fools. We may have escaped from their bottle prison—but we'll never escape *them.* They're everywhere."

Old Ivy stared at Mother. "You've been imprisoned by *giants?*"

"Indeed." Uncle scowled, but there was a hint of pride in his voice. "The giants invaded our riverbank colony and imprisoned us in a glass bottle. Yes, *bottle.*" He snorted the word. "Evil glassy stuff. But we escaped; we made it to this land. And now we find . . . more giants." His fist thumped the branch fiercely. "There is no place safe from the beasts! Not one bush—one tree—"

"There is a place." Old Ivy spoke slowly. Her wrinkled face was pale as she stared at Uncle, then at the rest of them. "You can escape the giants' colony—if you cross the grassland." She pointed through the leaves to a far-off mountain, like a gray-white blur in the distance.

"On the other side of that stone mountain—lies the river."

V

The Forbidden Lands

River.

Beyond the giants' grassland and past the great mountain was the river.

Ripple's head buzzed. Too much had happened too fast. She could hardly think.

The wonderful splashing water she'd thought she'd never see again was out there. Just waiting for them, on the other side of this grassland.

They could go there; they could *go* to the river!

"I can't believe it," Mother said for the third

time. "The *river!*"

"Tell me about this river." Crick swung restlessly on an overhanging branch. "I've never even seen one."

"Oh, Crick!" Ripple cried. "The river is . . . is. . . ." She looked at him helplessly. How could she even begin to describe the wonders of the riverbank colony where she and Mother and Uncle Kane had lived? The fun of splashing along the edges of the water with the other children; the excitement of watching the fishermen haul in their catch; the thrilling adventures of the scouts who protected their colony. Of course, there had been danger there, too. Ripple's own father had lost his life on a scouting expedition. Still, the river had always been a friend, a lively splashing presence.

Crick couldn't understand. He and Pan and Lissa had lived in some place called Garden before giants captured them and put them in the bottle. Ripple had talked to Crick and Lissa about many things since she'd first met them in that bottle. But how could she tell them about the magic of the river? She gave up trying to find words.

"You'll see," she promised. "You'll see how wonderful it is when we get there."

Crick peered out through the branches. "If we

fly, it shouldn't take too long to cross the grass-land." Then he looked at Ripple and frowned. "Well, no; we can't all fly. You haven't got them yet, have you?" he said bluntly, as if it were the first time he'd really thought about it.

Ripple turned away quickly, tossing her head.

"Do you think everyone gets them at the same time?" she said, trying to ignore the tight knot in her stomach.

"It's because she's been sick," Lissa said quickly. "That's why it's taking her longer."

"Right," Crick agreed cheerfully. "You'll probably get them any time now."

"Sure. Any time now." Ripple tossed her head again, aware that both Mother and Pan were look-ing at her with concern. Inside, the knot of fear pulled tighter. What if . . . what if the magic didn't come? What if a horrible hump like Old Ivy's grew on her back instead? And she had to spend the rest of her life hobbling around?

"When can we start across, then?" Crick pulled at leaf bits impatiently. "There are giants out there now."

"The giants leave the grassland at night," Old Ivy said. "When I need grasses for weaving, I go into the grassland and pick them at night. I'll wait here with you till nightfall. Then you can cross and I will go back to my shelter."

Uncle rose. "What kind of cowards do you take us for, woman!" he exploded. "We wouldn't for one *second* consider leaving you behind on such a trip. You are coming with us. The matter is settled!"

"The matter is not settled!" Old Ivy snapped back. "I have a perfectly good home in my thornbush, and I haven't the slightest intention of galloping across the grasslands!"

Ripple stared at Old Ivy curiously. Didn't the humped old woman really care if the rest of them left her in that can-shelter? Didn't she care if she had only creepers to talk to? Ripple felt uneasy thinking about it. It wasn't that she really *liked* the sharp-tongued old woman. . . .

She heard whispering behind her and turned to see Mother and Pan talking in low voices, farther down the branch, their heads close together. Ripple stood very still, straining to hear.

" . . . not good."

"That mountain is high. How can she—"

"She's been sick." Mother's voice. Low, intense. "It'll *come*."

They were whispering about her. Ripple reached back once again to touch the empty space between her shoulders. She stared out across the grassland, at the shadowy far-off mountain. It was hard to tell from here how high it was; the gray-white color seemed to blend into the cloudy sky. Even so, it looked very high.

How could she cross such a mountain without wings? And how could they manage to cross the entire grassland on foot? She would hold the rest of them back. The longing and the worry poured over her, as powerful as her homesickness for the river.

"Magic," she whispered desperately in her mind, "come. Please come!"

"Old Ivy's right. The giants do leave at night," Ripple reported, staring out at the shadowed grassland. "I don't hear any stomping now."

"Tie up your seed pouch," Mother ordered. "We don't know what we'll find when we get to that mountain." She picked up here spear, stepping around Uncle, who was snoring in a corner under the bush. "And we don't really know what kind of a place it is out there." Her voice dropped; she nodded toward the dark grasses. "We must be prepared for anything—have weapons, food. I wish you children were more trained in camouflage. . . ."

Ripple tried to listen respectfully; tried hard not to show her impatience. If Mother got into one of her organizing moods, they might never get going on the journey.

Pan pulled out a lantan weed and stood a moment, chewing, staring at the grasses. "I stayed up in the bush for a while, after the rest of you climbed down," he said. "Two giants came quite close to my hiding place. I tried to listen to them." He shook his head. "Most of their talk made no sense to me. About the only thing I understood was that they call this place 'park.'"

"Park?" Ripple echoed the strange new word. "I wonder what it means."

Old Ivy stood up. "Did you say you *listened* to those giants? That you understood their babblings?" Her voice was incredulous.

"Pan knows a lot of things about giants," Mother said proudly. "He lived in a garden near giants once; he learned some of their words. When we were imprisoned in the bottle forest, he listened to them through the glass—so we could plan our escape."

Old Ivy shook her head in wonder. "Who would have thought that the great beasts could *talk*," she murmured in a tone of disbelief. "Or that the giants had such a prison called 'bottle'; and that you *escaped* from it. . . ."

"The giants are gone now. Let's get going!" Crick cried, hopping up into an impatient glide, over the grasses. "Come on!" he called back. Then he landed abruptly, staring up toward the sky.

"Diy! Look up there! Did the giants put the moon on a pole?"

Ripple hurried toward where he was standing. She craned her neck, staring past the grasses. And for the first time she saw the great high pole rising above the grassland like a tree trunk, with a round glowing ball of light on the top.

"A pole-moon," Lissa breathed, behind her. "Can even giants do such a thing?"

"*The forbidden lands!*" Uncle stood beside them suddenly, fully awake, his eyebrows drawn together in a fierce frown, his walking stick raised.

"I have heard of such a place as this," he hissed, waving his stick at the grassland, the pole-moon. "It is in the old tales: a place of high grasses, of strange moonlight glowing from a pole. A place of danger and wickedness!" He seemed suddenly twice as tall, standing there full of authority and wisdom and dark knowledge. The elder. "The forbidden lands!" he repeated fiercely. "We must turn back!"

Ripple gulped. She felt a shiver of fear, looking out at the grasses, dark with night shadows, and the strange pole-moon glowing above them. Was there some unseen evil in those grasses, that place? Uncle knew. He knew all the old tales.

"But . . . but . . . " she whispered. "We have to cross, to reach the river."

"Yes," Crick cried, "we can't turn back now!"

"I tell you, it's an evil place!" Uncle pounded his walking stick against the ground. "We will not set foot or wing in there!"

"Poppy-rot," Old Ivy said. She faced Uncle, hands on her hips. "Poppy-rot," she said again. "There is no more danger there than any other place in this land."

Ripple gasped. Such a thing! To confront Uncle Kane in his authority as elder. Uncle's mouth had dropped open.

"Silence, woman!" he thundered. "You do not know the old tales!"

They glared at each other a second. Two spots of color came into Ivy's cheeks. "But I know the grasslands," she said evenly. "I have crossed on foot. And I have picked grasses there many times. Like this." And she started forward with quick determined steps, pushing into the grasses.

"By all the gods and pioneers!" Uncle called irritably, thrashing after her. "Stay away from there, I tell you!"

Old Ivy just moved faster, plucking the smaller grass blades, thrusting them into her cape pocket. And Uncle charged in right after her, still yelling in a fierce whisper:

"Come back, stubborn woman! Get your cursed grass somewhere else!"

The rest of them just stood there, stunned,

watching the incredible scene. Pan spoke first.

"That uncle of yours is as unpredictable as the giants themselves," he said to Mother, throwing up his arms. "And Ivy is no better." Then he reached for his spear and started after them.

"We can't lose sight of them!" Mother rose into the air, gliding past him.

"Maybe by the time Uncle catches up with Old Ivy, they'll be across the grassland." Crick grinned.

Ripple giggled at the thought of Uncle puffing along, whispering his fierce "Come back, come back" over the whole great expanse of the grassland. Then her smile faded, as Crick, too, jumped into a glide.

Wings! She wanted them! She needed them!

"Ripple, come on. Let's catch up with them." Lissa stood just ahead of her, holding out her hand. Loyal Lissa. Ripple gave her a grateful look, then grabbed her hand. Together they plunged through the grasses.

The sky was cloudy; the air, heavy. There were no real moon or stars out. But the strange pole-moon of the giants cast an eerie glow over the whole land.

Ripple looked away from the glowing light, suddenly afraid. What if Uncle was right? What if there was some evil here? It was easy to believe it in this strange half-darkness, with the heavy feeling in the air, and the huge giants' contraptions throwing strange shadows everywhere.

"I wonder what the old tales say about this place," Lissa whispered. So she felt it, too. "All those big . . . things. And that pole-moon."

"Uncle's caught up with Old Ivy," Crick reported, swooping along beside them. "He's still yelling. She's still pulling grasses as fast as she can. Don't know who's going to win. They're just up ahead."

Ripple couldn't see them, but as she and Lissa pushed farther into the grasses, it was not hard at all to tell where the others were.

"By Nimrod, if you're so determined to come

out here, then come all the way with us, to the river!" Uncle's voice bellowed. "And that's the end of it!"

Ripple's jaw dropped in surprise. Uncle had completely changed his argument! Pan was right. Uncle Kane was absolutely unpredictable today!

"There they are," Lissa pointed, pulling Ripple with her into a small clearing, where the others were watching Uncle and Old Ivy.

"I will pick my grasses," Old Ivy was saying in a slow, angry tone, "and then I will go back to my own home. My home is—" She stopped, as a sudden loud rumble boomed across the grassland.

"Giants?"

"Are the giants coming back?"

"No." Old Ivy's voice was oddly hoarse. She stood as rigid as a branch, her eyes wide and wild.

"That rumble came from the sky."

VI

Ivy's Story

A great flash of light tore open the sky. There was another deep, warning rumble. The grasses began to wave in the wind.

"Thunderstorm!"

"Back to the bush!"

"No—there's not time!"

Another rumble. It shook the earth and sky. The wind whistled across the grasstops.

"*Run!*"

The fear was alive, humming around their heads like a wind, making their voices shrill.

Thunderstorm—with hard, killing winds that shredded the wings, flooded the low shelters, split trees with ragged light flashes, and roared through the world like an angry monster.

"Over there!" Mother yelled, pointing to one of the giants' contraptions, rising out of the grasses. "We can hide under it." She grasped Uncle's arm. "Hurry!"

"Right," Pan yelled back. "Everyone under

that thing." He caught at Old Ivy's arm as she started running in the opposite direction. "No!" he shouted at her. "There's no time for you to go back! This is closer!"

The grasses whipped wildly about them. They raced toward the towering platform. There was dirt beneath it, not grass; dirt that sloped down in a valley, then rose back up. They reached it just as the rain started falling.

Ripple collapsed on the hilly ground, panting, gasping, rubbing her leg. The wild, panicky run had started it throbbing again.

The rain sounded like a million rocks falling on the shiny hard platform roof above them. Which one of the giants' objects was this? It couldn't be the long plank that went up and down, or the swinging-seats. Was it the round one, then? She lay there, trying to catch her breath, staring up at the platform.

She nudged Crick. "Is this the thing the giants went around and around on?" she whispered.

He nodded, still panting.

"Old Ivy," Mother sounded worried, "are you . . . all right?"

The old woman was sitting in a still, tight ball, arms hugging her drawn-up knees, fists clenched. She stared blankly at Mother, as if she hadn't really heard.

"You look ill." Uncle frowned. "Maybe you should lie down."

She held up her hand, shaking her head angrily. "Leave me be." Then she drew her cape tighter about her.

The rain fell harder, pouring over the edges of the platform in an angry waterfall, slanting in toward them, as the wind blew sideways.

"Diy!" Crick sounded miserable. "We'll be flushed out like worms if this keeps up."

"Sh!" Lissa hissed at him. "No use talking like that." She pushed her dripping hair back and turned to Uncle. "When the giants tried to poison us back in the bottle forest, and we had to go underground, you told us legends." She put her hand on his knee. "It helped us forget the danger. Can you do that now?"

Uncle looked at her. He fingered his bushy beard, stared past them into the wet angry world of the storm.

"Thunderstorms have troubled our people—the Micarus—since the beginnings of our history," he began slowly, with a far-off look in his eyes. He sat up straighter.

"And not only the first pioneers, but every generation." His voice grew deeper, louder.

"I remember when I was a young boy. There was an especially violent spring storm one year.

The river rose over its banks. We managed to climb to safety—all but one boy. He lost his footing and fell, hurting his leg.

"There was no time to lose. The river was rising very fast." Uncle's voice swelled with drama. His eyes burned. Uncle was a different person when he got deep into a story.

"The elders of the colony grabbed a fishing net and tied rope to it. A scout climbed down with it and got the boy inside. They pulled the lad up in the net, just ahead of the rising water."

Uncle fingered his beard, still staring past them with that faraway story look. "I can remember it all so clearly. Even the boy's face. His name was . . ." He paused. "His name was. . . ."

"Reed." Old Ivy stood up, staring at Uncle. She spoke like someone in a daze. "The boy's name was Reed."

Uncle's mouth opened in a big "O", then shut, then opened again. He stood up slowly, pointing a suddenly trembling finger at Old Ivy.

"You . . . you . . . how . . . " he stammered. "You . . . but. . . ."

Mother stared, her hand tight on Pan's arm. "But how. . . ." And her voice, too, faded off.

Crick said it. "How did you know the boy's name, unless, unless—" He looked from Old Ivy to Uncle and back again. His eyes widened.

"I will tell you a story now." Old Ivy's voice was low and harsh. "It is the story of a young girl. She was alone on a weed-gathering trip. She went too far from her colony. Then"—Old Ivy took a deep breath—"the wind came up. A storm. Hard wind, driving rain. There was no way for her to make it back to her colony in the storm. She tried to take shelter in a bush. It was a bad idea. The wind caught at her and blew her about like a leaf, first one way and then another, tumbling her high, then tossing her toward the ground.

"Then," Old Ivy's voice was a hoarse croak, "a flash of light from the sky split a tree overhead. Branches fell everywhere. One fell on her, crushing her wings, twisting her back."

The old woman's fingers pulled hard at the strings of her cape. She took another deep breath.

"When the storm stopped, the girl managed to crawl under a bush. She stayed there a long time. She drank from a water puddle left by the storm. She ate leaves scattered nearby. After a while her strength came back. But not her wings. They were gone for that season. For all seasons."

"Diy," Crick whispered, wide-eyed. Then again, "*Diy!*"

"The storm had tossed her over the great stone mountain. And so—she made her home here—on this side of the mountain."

She stopped.

There was silence. Ripple felt shivers shoot like pieces of ice through her body. Such a disaster was a hundred times worse than anything that the rest of them had been through.

Uncle's face looked very peculiar. He stumbled over to Old Ivy. "You—" he said hoarsely. "You . . . " he tried again. "The . . . weaver girl. Daughter of Niran. The one who . . . never came back." He shook his head, wiped his forehead, dropped heavily onto the dirt, as if his legs had suddenly given out. "By all the heroes," he muttered, "how can it be?"

Mother took a step forward.

"One of the . . . lost ones." Her voice was not very steady. "From our colony. . . ." She was staring at Old Ivy as if she had never seen her before.

Ripple sat frozen. Her head buzzed like a drone-creature. Old Ivy was one of them. A Moth-Kin. From *their* river.

VII

The Mudland

"Old Ivy *has* to come with us, to the river," Lissa said fiercely. "There must be some way to convince her."

"If any of us ever gets out of here." Crick paced restlessly back and forth. "If that storm ever stops." He glanced over at Uncle, stretched out on high, dry land, snoring. "How can he sleep in all this racket?"

Ripple knew she could never sleep. Not with the awful noise outside: clattering raindrops, howling wind, splashing water. Her leg throbbed from the fast, hard run, and her head throbbed with new thoughts and new ideas from this strange night.

"*Our* river. We're going toward *our* river," she told herself for the fiftieth time, hugging her knees to her chin. And Old Ivy was one of them. The incredible thoughts roared through her head in a storm of their own.

Somehow they would cross the treacherous grassland. Somehow they would climb that great faraway mountain. And then—the river! The excitement was too great. She would never be able to sleep, even if they had to stay here all night.

The next thing she knew, Mother was bending over her, shaking her shoulders. "Ripple, get up."

She jerked awake. There was a great wad of leaves plastered to her leg with mud. She tried to shake it off.

"Medicine leaves." Old Ivy came over to her. "They were in my cape pocket." She scowled down at Ripple. "You overdid it on that leg, you know."

Ripple opened her mouth to give back a sharp answer, then closed it. She looked at the old woman, confused. Ivy sounded as irritable as ever, but—she had taken time to fix that mud pack. And it had helped. This morning there was no pain at all in her leg. And, after all, Old Ivy was one of them.

"Th . . . ank you," Ripple said finally.

"Mud," Pan said behind her. "Everywhere."

Ripple stood up quickly. "What?"

"The storm finally stopped." Mother's voice was grim. "And it left us surrounded by mud."

Squish Splat Splosh!

Mud flew at them, splattering their tunics, their faces.

"What's happening?"

"*Diy!*"

"By all the pioneers—"

There was a great *Bonnnggg* overhead, followed by an earsplitting *Creeaakk*. The great platform over their heads began to spin.

"Great Nimrod, the sky's falling!"

"Down everyone. Way down," Pan cried, grabbing Mother's hand and pulling her down with him. Ripple pressed close to the ground, her hands over her ears, trying to drown out the awful noise of the whirling platform.

Oh, no. Oh, no. She looked at Lissa, then Crick.

"A giant's up there." Crick's mouth formed the words, but Ripple couldn't hear them.

"I know," she mouthed back. "I know."

Even with her ears covered, the next *bonnnggg* practically lifted her off the ground. Then another *splat, splosh, splattt*, flinging more mud at them. Then, silence.

They crouched against the ground a moment longer, as the platform overhead spun slower and slower and finally was still.

Their tight control exploded. Everyone yelling.

"A giant! It was a giant on the platform!"

"It's gone now. And we'd better be gone, too— before the next one comes!"

"Another attack." Uncle's face was gray. "We

are doomed. I told you it was a mistake to come to this cursed place! But did anyone listen?" He glared at Ivy.

"We've got to get across this mud." Pan looked at Mother, then at Ripple. And Ripple's stomach suddenly felt as heavy as if it, too, had filled with mud during the night. How could she—or Ivy—cross the oozing mudland without wings?

"Here! Over here," Crick yelled. He had run part way around the huge central pole that held up the platform. "It's higher ground. There's not so much mud." He looked at Ripple as he spoke. "It's not much more than a jump. Really."

The others ran toward him. Pan grasped Old Ivy around the shoulders, half-pulling her along. "You can't stay here now. None of us can."

"You just listen to me—I am staying here until the ground dries. The rest of you can go on."

Mother's arm tightened around Ripple's shoulders. "If everyone helps, we can all make it across."

"But . . . but. . . ." Ripple felt a great lump of fear clog her throat as she stared across the mud, where Crick was pointing.

She could never jump that far.

"You're *what*? No, it's not possible!" Old Ivy's voice, half-commanding, half-pleading. "*Let go of me!*"

Ripple wasn't sure exactly what happened next.

There was a confused tangle of arms reaching out, voices shouting—then Mother's and Crick's arms grasping her under the armpits.

A great leap into the air, a feeling of swift exhilaration that changed to terror when the momentum from her jump was gone—and the only thing keeping her in the air was Crick's and Mother's hard-straining wingbeats.

It was a second; it was an hour; it was a slow-motion world. The grass, just beyond reach; the mud drawing closer, trying to grab her toes . . . Crick and Mother breathing hard.

"Higher!" she screamed and drew her legs up to her chest in terror. Her heart was trying to jump the rest of the way by itself.

Were Pan and Lissa and Uncle keeping Old Ivy up?

Ripple shut her eyes. She felt the slime close over her toes. Then the rest of her body hit hard ground, as they crashed in a heap onto the grasses just beyond the mudhole.

VIII

The Sign of the Sunstalk

Green grass stalks slapped Ripple's face, jabbed her arms, her legs, shaking great water drops over her, as she collapsed on the wet ground.

"Mmmmade it." Crick flung himself down.

"Careful," Mother gasped. "It's wet here, too."

"Such . . . a . . . thing." Old Ivy spaced the words out with each breath. "Grabbed, yanked, hauled. . . ." She glared at all of them, then took a deep breath and closed her eyes.

"Even the first pioneers—" But Uncle was too winded to finish. He hunched over, wheezing.

"But we made it." Crick sat up and took a deep breath. He looked over at Ripple and grinned, a cocky triumphant grin.

"Hardly more than a jump. Just like I said."

Ripple tried to fix her expression into a stern glare.

"Sure. Sure," she wanted to say. "See how *you* like dragging your toes in the mud and having your arms yanked out." Instead, she felt the corners of her mouth slowly turn up in a reluctant, answering grin. They *had* made it over the treacherous mud and into a land of glistening grass. The high stalks completely enclosed them in a world of green. Since they had come out on a different side of the giants' great platform, Ripple had completely lost her sense of direction.

"Which way do we go? Where are we?"

"When we find that out, I'm heading back for my own bush," Ivy declared.

"Oh, quiet, woman," Uncle growled irritably.

"We're right in the middle of the giants' grassland. We need to find some shelter." Pan jumped into a low glide, hovering above the grasstops. "The giants will be back."

"You can count on that," Uncle muttered.

"Don't look at me for ideas," Old Ivy snapped. "You got yourselves into this mess. I didn't ask to be hauled like a sack of seeds across the mud. If you will recall, I had planned to stay safely under that platform, not causing anyone any trouble." Ripple knew what Old Ivy was thinking. With only Ripple to carry, they could manage much better.

Crick flew up to join Pan.

"What about that bush?" he cried, pointing.

"There's a giant's contraption over there, too," Pan answered. "We'll have to be careful."

"Which is the way back to my thornbush?" Old Ivy asked them.

"Ivy, you can't go back that way, alone, in broad daylight!" Mother cried. "We can't let you!"

"Ridiculous to try," Uncle declared. "Suicidal."

"Come with us—at least as far as that bush Crick saw," Lissa pleaded.

Ivy looked at all of them. She drew her cape closer. "I'll come with you as far as the bush," she said unsmilingly. "Only that far. At night I leave."

"Want me to fly ahead and scout that bush?" Crick called.

"No!" There was a sharpness in Mother's voice. "There'll be no more wandering off—by *anybody*. We'll all stay together."

"Flying's not safe here anyway. No overhead cover and too many birds in the sky." Pan landed beside them. "The giants could come back any minute. We're wasting time here."

They started hiking through the grass. A few moments later, Ripple pointed to a great plump stalk just visible through the grasses. "Look, everyone!" she cried excitedly. "It's a sunstalk!" She ran toward it.

Back at the riverbank, sunstalks had meant good luck. The round flowerheads always started out yellow, like the sun. Then, when the flower's time of magic came, it changed into hundreds of white cloud puffs that sailed away like wings. The first person to spot a white flowerhead and shake down the white tufts would be covered with luck.

> "Sunstalk so tall
> Let the magic fall!"

She chanted the familiar tune the children of the colony had always sung. This stalk had already lost a lot of its tufts, probably in the storm. Ripple shook the stalk, trying to coax down the ones that were left. At first, nothing happened. The cloud puffs were wet and stubborn. She shook harder. Two white tufts sailed down. One landed on Lissa's arm and stuck there. The other clung to Ripple's hair.

"Let the magic fall!" Ripple chanted again, shaking with all her might. And the last tufts broke loose from the stalk and fell like snow over them all.

"Now we're all covered with the sunstalk's magic wings!" Ripple cried. "It's our good luck sign for crossing the grasslands." Then in a whisper, "Especially me, sunstalk. Please bring magic to me."

She looked up to find Mother's eyes on her.

"It will come, daughter." Mother's arm went around her shoulders. She looked at Ripple, then over at Ivy, then in the direction of the far-off mountain. She took a deep breath. "It *will.*"

"*Ah-choooo!*" Uncle's explosive sneeze would have blown all the white tufts back into the air again, if they weren't stuck to his wet clothes.

"You've caught a chill, Uncle," Mother worried.

"No." Crick grinned. "He's allergic to good luck."

Uncle scowled. "I'll tell you what I'm allergic to, young man. Giants. Giants' contraptions, giants' bottles, giants' grasslands, giants' mud!" He sneezed again. "Miserable nose," he groaned. "Cursed sneezing is wearing me out!"

"If you're tired, we can rest," Old Ivy said.

Uncle stared back at her. Then, to Ripple's surprise, he drew himself up, straightening his tunic, clearing his throat loudly.

"No," he declared, sliding into his deep voice, "we must press onward, toward our destination!" And he strode after Pan, into the grasses.

Crick nudged Ripple. "I do believe Uncle's trying to impress Old Ivy," he whispered, with a wicked grin.

Ripple grinned back. Then, impulsively, she rumpled her hair into an imitation of Uncle's wild mane and stuck out her stomach.

"We must press onward!" she cried in her best Uncle voice. Then she held her finger under her nose. "*Ah-ah-ah-choooo!*"

Crick and Lissa clapped their hands over their mouths to hold in the laughter. Ripple bowed. No one could "do" people as well as she could.

Was it the sunstalk's lucky tufts, still clinging to her wet tunic, that made her feel suddenly light and venturesome? Or was it the sight of the sun shining on the wet grasses? Or the fact that there were as yet no more giants stomping about, shaking the earth? Or the memory of Mother's firm voice promising, "It will come"?

She picked up a stick from the ground and grasped it firmly. "We're scouts, Crick and Lissa," she said eagerly. For the first time, she felt caught up in the thrill of this new adventure. They *were* scouts, journeying through a strange green grass forest filled with raindrops that sparkled in the sun, making their way past great dangers, as they headed toward the dark shadow of the mountain in the distance.

It didn't matter that the rain had turned half the grassland into mudholes, just waiting for one unwary step. She had conquered one mudhole today—she would conquer them all!

Scouts knew how to avoid the muck, to find patches of firm ground to step on, to keep eyes and ears alert, watching for death-webs, pincers, stingers, birds overhead. Scouts knew how to silently blend into the grasses when enemies appeared.

I'm learning! Ripple thought with a quick burst of pride. She wasn't as good as Old Ivy, who moved as silently as a breeze in the grasses, or as quick as Pan or Mother, but she was learning. And it wasn't just scary. It was exciting. "Our river," she told herself. "We're heading toward our river!"

A sudden thought struck her. "Mother, are there other rivers like ours?"

Mother hesitated. "I don't know, Ripple. I used to think our river was the only one in the world. I used to think it *was* the world. But now I've learned differently from Pan."

Pan turned at the sound of his name. "Learned what from Pan?" he asked teasingly.

Mother snatched the lantan weed out of his mouth. "Learned to hate that filthy weed," she shot back. But she was smiling her special Pan-smile that smoothed all the worry lines from her face.

A look passed between Pan and Mother. Crick nudged Ripple.

"Good thing Uncle Kane is an elder," he whispered, with a mischievous grin. "He'll be needing to do a marrying ceremony for those two for sure!"

"Blasted mudholes. Infernal muck!" Uncle didn't share the good mood of the others at all. He shook a slime-covered weed from his tunic with a look of disgust. "Cursed giants' land!"

"At least they're gone for now," Ripple said to cheer him up. "Maybe they won't be back today. Maybe they don't like mud, either."

"They'll be back," Pan said grimly. "They don't give up so easily. And we must be ready for their next trick."

Lissa spoke.

"They caught us once;
But—no more.
We shall outwit them,
And reach the river shore."

There was a quiet fierceness in her voice.

Uncle's scowl disappeared. He stared at Lissa. "You, Lissa, have the gift of the storyteller. You must not forget any of this. You will be the one to tell this story."

"Our story," Ripple whispered. "Our journey back to the river."

And then, abruptly, the grass ended. They stood facing a gigantic plank of wood, lying like a wall in front of them.

IX

The Giants' Plank

They stared up at the huge, sloping plank that crushed the grass at one end and rose up to meet the sky at the other.

"We must have veered. . . ." Mother looked around in confusion.

"I'll take a look and see." Crick jumped up, landing in one graceful glide on top of the plank.

"Have you gone crazy!" Uncle roared up at him. "Dancing like a little fool on top of that cursed thing!"

Crick grinned down at him, his hands on his waist.

"The view's great!" he called down. "And it's *dry*. No muck!"

"Dry, is it?" Uncle asked in a completely different tone. He fingered his beard, staring up at the plank. "No mud?"

Pan turned to Mother. "This must be the plank that the giants went up and down on. Remember? There was a giant sitting at each end."

While the others talked, Ripple sat down on the ground. Strange—but suddenly all the energy had drained out of her body, leaving her muscles so tired, they ached. Was she still weak from the bite, even though the pain in her leg was gone?

"Come on up, slowpoke!" Crick called down to her. She looked up to see all of them on the plank already, even Uncle. Old Ivy was hoisting herself up.

"Here, I'll help pull you up, Ripple." Crick leaned over, holding out his arm.

The plank wasn't so much higher than she was. But it seemed to take a lot of effort to climb up; Crick had to practically haul her over the edge. By the time Ripple made it onto the plank, there was a humming in her ears. She felt angry with herself; one little hike shouldn't have worn her out so quickly!

"Isn't the view great?" Lissa said in wonder. "You can see everything!"

"There's the platform we hid under. How *huge* it is," Mother said.

"There's the bush I told you about." Crick pointed. "It's not far."

Ripple took a deep breath, trying to clear the light-headed feeling. Then she looked around. Crick was right. The view was great. She could see the grass tops waving around her in all directions; see the enormous giants' contraptions—the platform, the swinging seat-things, and the tall, shiny hill. And beyond all that stood the great stone mountain. It was her first good clear look at it.

The mountain seemed to stretch from one end of the earth to the other. Straight, sheer, unending, as if cut from one gigantic rock. Impossibly high.

"Wall." Pan's voice spoke behind her. He was staring at the mountain, too.

"What?" Mother asked.

"Wall," he said again. "There was a stone mountain like that in the garden where we used to live. I didn't recognize what it was before; we were too far away. The giants called it 'wall'."

"It's so steep," Mother murmured.

It wasn't just tiredness that caused the sudden horrible sinking feeling in Ripple's stomach. That mountain was much too straight and high to climb.

No one could ever cross it . . . without wings.

Ripple's throat burned as they all stood staring at the mountain. All except Uncle. Through a blur, Ripple heard his voice.

"We'll just rest here a few minutes. . . ." Uncle sounded more pleasant than he had all day. He patted the plank with a sigh. "Ah, dry wood. Wonderful dry wood. Have you got any more seeds, Fern?" He stretched out with another sigh. "Things are looking better. Giants are gone. We've crossed about a third of the way; we may get across this grassland yet—" Then he jumped up, toppling into Crick.

"Dear sweet Nimrod," he croaked. "A giant. Coming right at us!"

X

The Magic

Three things happened.

The giant charged toward them.

A terrific shudder ripped through the plank. It jerked below them in a tremendous hard jolt.

And they were hurtling through the sky.

Ripple heard a scream. Was it her own? No, it couldn't be. She couldn't see, couldn't hear, couldn't breathe. She was a numb body shooting through the spinning sky.

This was it. The giant had hurled them to their death, catapulted them to the very top of the heavens.

Higher, higher, faster, faster.

"Flying. I'm flying." The crazy thought spun dizzily through her brain. "First flight . . . without wings . . . no magic."

And then, suddenly, the great force that had shot them upward had spent itself. For a split second she hung suspended in midair. Then she started to drop.

Green rushed toward her. A great mass of green: pricking, jabbing, crackling, bending.

A hard, whooshing jolt.

And the world stopped whizzing past.

Or was it she who had stopped?

The humming in her head was worse. It took a lot of effort to open her eyes. It was even harder to think, to try and make sense of the green leaves all around her.

Had she fallen in a bush? A tree? Where were the others?

She would find out. She would sit up, look around, get her bearings . . . in a minute.

She shut her eyes again. It felt so good just to lie still in the soft cushion of leaves, to let her body relax, her mind relax. Not to run from anything. Not to fight anything.

The humming was stronger in her head. It dipped and rose, almost in a tune. It seemed to wrap a spell around her. When she tried to open one eye, all she could see was gray, like fog, or shadows.

Everything felt warm and soft. And the humming in her head was nice, too. It *was* a tune, lulling her. There was a funny smell in the air. A strange, sharp scent.

She didn't mind.

For now she would let the gray fog wrap itself around her. She could float in the lovely feeling forever, let the humming go on and on, like a sleepy lullaby. . . .

But something was wrong.

An itch. That was it. Somewhere on her back. She would have to reach back to scratch it, if she could wake up, unwrap herself from the gray fog.

At first her arm wouldn't obey. But the itching got worse. She tried to move, to turn, to fight through the fog. It was too much work. If it wasn't for that itch—

She struggled harder. The fog was too tight now; it was suffocating her, more a prison than a lovely floating bed.

She fought, thrashing out for air, room, light. Her arms were free. Her legs were free.

She squinted. Slowly things came into focus. She saw leaves, branches.

A tree. She was on the branch of a tree.

But something felt different. Her back. . . .

She reached behind her, heart pounding. Her fingers felt the membranes, still shiny-wet with newness.

The magic! It had come!

She stood up on the branch. She sat down. She stood up again. She turned around, craning her neck to see. Her smile reached both ears. Joy was a waterfall tumbling through her body.

The magic! The poison of the insect-beast hadn't destroyed her power for magic after all! She wasn't doomed to stay on the ground. The wings had just taken longer to come. And this strange dream-night had been the night of her magic!

The dizziness, the heavy, tired feeling—it hadn't just been the shock of shooting through the air and falling into a tree.

"I've got them! I've got them!" she whispered joyfully, jumping into an experimental hop-flight. The sunstalk had brought her good luck after all. The best kind of luck. The magic! She craned her neck for another glimpse of the wondrous wings, shimmering in the early morning light.

So—the change had taken all night. She wasn't tired. Far from it. The power and strength of the magic burned through her like fire. She could hardly wait to show the others.

The others! The thought hit like a splash of cold water. Where were they?

The magical change had driven all other thoughts and worries from her mind. Now she looked around in panic. Were they somewhere in this tree, too?

She would find them. The magic would help her. She took a step forward and shook her body a little to dry off the extra moisture. Something inside her knew. . . .

The wings spread.

It was a different world. A world of green and gold leaves that rustled and crackled, of sunlight slanting in between the branches, of air currents that carried her along, and wind that roughened her flight, of many layered branchways, some dark and narrow, others wide and arching. She maneuvered through them, dipping, searching, listening.

The others would be here. They had to be here. And she would find them. Nothing could go wrong on this time of her first magic.

Of course they were all right. After all, they could fly.

Except Old Ivy.

Suddenly the great, bubbly, happy feeling was gone. A picture floated through her mind, a pic-

ture of the wrinkled humped old woman, tumbling
through the air helplessly, her cape blowing
around her. The thought sent a surprisingly sharp
stab of fear through her.

"Old Ivy," she whispered, and beat her wings
harder—searching more branchways, far into the
top height of the tree, then circling, swerving,

doubling back for spots she might have missed. Back and forth. Around and up and down—

It was Uncle's voice that led her to them finally.

"Vile loathsome creatures!"

Ripple swerved, searching the branches below, frantically.

"They will stop at nothing! There's no telling what they've done with her!"

Ripple dived toward the sound, swerving to avoid the snarling branchtips.

"We've searched and searched—called her and called her."

" . . . no answer."

There they were, on a wide branch below. All of them! Relief poured through her. And a glorious burst of pride.

"Here! Here!" she yelled, waving her arms.

And then, with a great thrill of triumph, she launched herself toward the incredulous upturned faces.

XI

The Special Power

"She's got them! She's got them!" Crick whooped. "Ripple's got wings, everyone!"

"Ripple—oh, Ripple!" Mother's hug made it almost impossible to breathe. "Ripple," she whispered again. She shook her head. "First the bite of the insect-beast and now this. I am not going to let you out of my sight for one second!" She held Ripple at arm's length and stared at her. Ripple noticed that Mother's arms were bruised and scratched, and there were great rips in her tunic.

"I told you it would come, Ripple," Lissa cried. "It just took longer, because of that bite."

"*Here*, of all places." Mother shook her head again. "Thank the Mighty One for your safe return. But at least you had the scent for protection."

"Scent?" Ripple looked at her, puzzled. Then she remembered the strange, sharp smell that had soaked through the shadows. "That smell is for protection?"

"Without it, we would be defenseless against enemies, lying there alone."

"Strange time you picked, Ripple." Pan had found a lantan somewhere. It dangled from the corner of his mouth as he stood watching her. His smile teased, but there was a warm look in his eyes. "While the rest of us were grabbing onto Ivy by her cape and crashing through the tree, falling through branches, and practically breaking our necks." Pan's arms had some nasty-looking scratches, too.

"Strange *place*." Something in Uncle Kane's voice made everyone turn to look at him. He walked over to Ripple; with each step he seemed to grow taller. Despite the new rips in his tunic, the matted beard, and the bruise below his eye, he was suddenly the elder.

"This girl . . . this girl"—he shook a trembling finger at Ripple—"has come into her magic in the very *depths* of the giants' land. Never in the history of our people has there been such a thing! Such a magic means something! It must carry a special power! It means—"

"It means that Ripple will be able to cross over the great mountain with you." Old Ivy's raspy voice was very calm, matter-of-fact. Her face, too was badly scratched. She limped a little as she turned to face Ripple. "Now you can reach the river. All of you."

Ripple looked down.

Her own magic had come. But Old Ivy's would never come. Old Ivy would never feel the power, the thrill, never hear the humming song, or smell that scent.

Ripple remembered the terrible bleak feeling inside her, watching Lissa's and the others' wings, when she had none. Her eyes went to Old Ivy's proud, stern face. Did Old Ivy feel like that?

I wasn't right. All her life Ripple had longed for the magic. And now, finally, it had come. And it wasn't enough.

Unless somehow she could *make* it be Ivy's magic, too.

"We'll carry you across, Old Ivy!" The words burst from her of their own will. "We can do it!" She looked around at the others eagerly. "There're six of us. It would work!"

"I've had enough yanking and dragging to last me for the rest of my life, thank you. No. All you need to do is to help me from this tree. I am quite capable of getting back across."

"It would work!" Ripple whirled to face the others. "We're strong!" The power of new magic still pulsed through her. Couldn't the others feel it? They could do it, if they all worked together.

"I don't know, Ripple." Mother frowned. "Any

weight at all drags down the flight. Remember when we carried you just that little way across the mud?"

"But there are *six* of us!"

Uncle rubbed his beard, frowning, too. "There never has been——" he began.

"Yes, there has been!" Now Lissa jumped to her feet. "Uncle, it was in your story, remember? You said they pulled that boy up the riverbank in a net."

"That was a riverbank. We're talking about a *mountain*," Crick reminded her. "And we don't even have a net, anyway." But even as he spoke, his quick, lively eyes were roving, searching.

"The cape!" he cried suddenly, staring at Old Ivy. "We could use that!"

"For a carry net, you mean?" Mother fingered the edges of the woven material. "Ye . . es, it's a strong fiber."

"Of course it's strong!"

"Ivy, do you think you could curl up inside, like this?" Ripple demonstrated eagerly.

Pan crouched down beside her. "Ivy, let's spread it out and see what we've got."

Old Ivy scowled. "I never asked to be dragged here," she said stonily. "And I certainly never said I wanted my cape turned into a mass of ropes and knots."

But no one was listening. They were all talking at once.

"Look, if we tie a grass rope here and here. . . . "

"Like a hammock!"

"Such a thing. . . . " Uncle seemed a little bewildered. "To try to *fly* all together like that—it will take special power."

"Special power!" Ripple echoed triumphantly. "Uncle, you said that getting my wings right here in the giants' land meant special power. Well, maybe it means this, Uncle!"

"Ripple's right, Old Ivy." Lissa knelt beside the old woman and took her hands. "The cape will work. I know it will. You can come with us back to the river. Please."

Old Ivy looked away, at the stone mountain in the distance. For a long moment she said nothing, just stared with a strange look on her face, as if she could see beyond it. But when she turned back to them, her face settled into a normal scowl. She yanked off her cape.

"And what do you know about netmaking?" she asked crossly. "With your knowledge of knots and fiber, I'll end up spattered in a thousand pieces in the grass below." She pulled a weed from the cape pocket and began tying it on, still scowling.

"This is the way to do it! If I'm to be carted around like a bag of seeds, I want secure knots!" Deftly, she wove the strands together into a stronger rope, then attached it to the edge of the cape.

Ripple looked from Lissa to Crick, then back to Ivy. The old woman was helping!

A slow smile spread over Pan's face. He put his arm around Mother's shoulders. "Tonight, then," he said. "The giants will be gone then." He nodded toward the great bodies stomping about below in the grassland. "We can cross tonight."

Uncle reached down and gathered an edge of the cape in his hand. "Tonight," he echoed, shaking it fiercely in front of Ivy's face, "the magic will come to you, too, old woman!"

XII

The Attack

"The giants haven't left yet!" Ripple cried in frustration, peering through a gap in the leaves. Nervousness and eagerness churned inside her until she felt ready to explode. Her glance swept the grassland. The stone mountain stared back at her, huge and gray and still very far away. The last and most difficult part of their long and dangerous journey.

But beyond *that*—the river! The longing was fierce. She could sense it out there, see it in her mind. And when the breezes were right, she could even smell it.

The sun was almost down. The cape-net was finished, with rope handles for them to grasp. If only the last giants would leave!

Crick climbed up beside her. "Look at those two giants over there. They're sliding down the shiny hill." He shook his head in amazement. "Why do they do that?"

Ripple thought aboout it. "Maybe they're trying to scare away some insect-beasts."

"Diy!" Crick hooted. "Giants don't have to worry about insect-beasts! They can step on them!"

"Well, maybe there are bigger insect-beasts somewhere," Ripple flung back. "And maybe the giants slide down into the grass to scare them away."

Crick still looked scornful. "If there were bigger insect-beasts around, we would have seen them by now."

"Don't be too sure about that," Pan said, gazing out over the grassland. "I'm sure there are a lot of things in this world we haven't seen yet."

"There's the giants' plank." Ripple pointed to the huge long contraption. Even now, giants were riding it, one on each end. Up and down. Up and down.

Suddenly she understood how they had gotten flung into the air. "A giant must have sat on one end," she said, thinking out loud. "It made the other end go up fast, and it shot us up. That's what happened!"

"Look at that giant," Lissa cried, pointing. A giant was running across the grass, holding a string-rope that was connected to a white thing. It flapped along above him in the wind.

"Is that the giant's wings?" Lissa whispered. "Do giants have wings, too?"

"Diy." Crick sounded impressed. "Those giants are so heavy that their wings can't lift them up. Only their wings fly; the rest of them stays on the ground."

Giants were unbelievable creatures. There was no doubt about it. Before, in the grasses, Ripple had only glimpsed an enormous leg or foot. Back in the bottle, she had seen their faces and hands. But now, from the height of the tree, for the first time she'd had the opportunity to take in the complete and awful hugeness of the giants.

And yet, looking down on them, she didn't feel quite so helpless and outsized. With her magic, she could be *higher* than the giants!

Impulsively, Ripple got up and started walking in a hulked-over stance, arms up, feet stomping the tree bark hard with each step.

"*I am a giant!*" she boomed. "I can trample down grasses, and make huge ugly contraptions, and I can step on anything with my big foot!"

Crick and Lissa started to giggle. But Uncle shook his head.

"Contraptions. Planks that go up and down. Spinning platforms. Giants with wings that fly by themselves." His voice was very calm, controlled. "And to think that I once lived a normal, comfortable life by the river, with the rest of our colony. Fished. Scouted. Told the great tales."

"And you shall tell them again, when we reach the river!" Lissa turned to him, eyes shining. "And Uncle—what a tale that will be!"

"It's time," Pan said tersely. He gestured toward the rope handles. "We'll need three on the front and three on the back. Timing is most important. We'll have to work together to stay balanced."

Ripple gulped, clenched and unclenched her

fists, trying to work off the nervousness. She stared down at the grassland. The strange pole-moon of the giants cast its yellow-white light over the place. But it was not the only light in the sky tonight.

Green and yellow lights were starting to flash across the grassland. On—off. On—off. On—off. Star gods, flying over the grasses, blinking their friendly taillights. Star gods, the one winged creature Ripple didn't fear.

"The star gods are flying tonight," she said softly. "They'll bring us good luck."

"Giants!" Old Ivy cut in, her voice sharp, urgent. She pointed through the leaves at the hulking dark shadows. "Two of them. Coming this way."

"What!"

"It's night! You said they went away at night!"

"That giant's got something in its hand," Crick cried.

"What—" Ripple strained to see better. Then her breath stopped. Her fingers dug into Mother's arm.

"Glass. . . ." She could hardly say the dreaded word. "It's a glass . . . bottle!"

After all the time she'd spent staring through the glass walls of the bottle forest, there could be no mistaking the dreadful clear, hard substance. It glowed in the pole-moonlight. Hairs rose along the back of her neck.

"No!"

"Are they going to imprison us again!" Lissa cried shrilly.

"Diy! They're chasing after the star gods!" Crick shouted. "They're putting *them* in the bottles."

"The *star gods!*"

"They can't put them in an awful bottle!" They all watched in horror as the giant raised its arm toward the blinking star gods. A great lump formed in Ripple's throat.

"Don't let them," she whispered. "Fly away, fast. Don't let them put you in a horrible bottle!"

"Sacrilege! Do the great beasts do nothing but stampede about day and night, putting innocent creatures inside glass prisons!" Uncle's eyes blazed. "Sacrilege, I say!"

"There are more giants coming!"

"More bottles!"

"They'll be after us next. It's not safe here!"

"Old Ivy, climb inside the cape. Hurry!"

They were all talking at once, crawling along the branch, gathering the ropes, getting in each others' way. Ripple's throat was too tight to swallow.

"Grab the handles!" Pan ordered.

There was no time to think, to plan their movements; just a frantic lift-off, as they launched themselves into the leaf-shadowed darkness beyond their limb. Ripple's heart pounded in her throat as she clutched the rough rope, working her wings furiously, trying to dodge the dark branches.

"Left!" Mother cried, as a branch snapped toward them. Ripple's foot scraped a sharp twig. Then another branch. It took some hair with it. There was a quick gasp from Lissa and a grunt from Pan as the cape-bag lurched sharply sideways.

"Cursed tree," Uncle wheezed.

More branches, leaves, twigs. More scratches, bumps, lurches. And then suddenly the leaves thinned to a great openness. And they were pitching through a dark sea of air, while giants rushed by on all sides.

XIII

The Star Gods

The invasion. Like a nightmare that kept coming back. First on the riverbank, the giants' great feet had trampled everything in sight. Then, during the escape from the bottle forest, the hideous feet had stomped all about them. They had barely escaped with their lives.

And now, again. Only this time it was an invasion of the air. This time it was not feet, but hands and arms, all about them, swinging, clutching, shattering the air currents. The darkness was their only protection. Ripple's fingers curled so tightly on the rope that the rough fiber cut her skin. The fear was like a bitter poison in her mouth, spreading through her whole body.

At least they didn't have taillights to signal to the giants where they were, like the star gods. It was bad enough that there were six of them flying so close together, like a big clumsy creature with a sack dangling below it.

A sack that was getting heavier and heavier.

There was no room for their wings to open properly, no rhythm to help keep them aloft. Ripple could feel the strength oozing out of her.

A giant rushed by. They lurched sharply in the sudden rush of wind, struggling like swimmers in stormy waters.

They dropped lower.

Ripple could see the stone mountain, gleaming white, far in the distance.

They would never make it. The air was not a glorious place of freedom now; it was a stormy sea with dangerous currents—and it was sucking them down.

"Won't . . . make . . . it," Pan's voice rasped. "Land on . . . that."

A tall giants' contraption loomed before them out of the darkness. Ripple hardly saw it before they tumbled down on the cold, hard surface with a thud that knocked the breath from her body.

She lay there, exhausted. Her wings felt limp, her shoulders ached, her palms burned. She tried to press close to the cold, hard thing, to melt against its shadow, to stay invisible to the giants. She could hear the hard breathing of the others, and occasional wheezes and moans from Uncle. Still she lay there.

Later, she didn't remember when Old Ivy climbed out of the cape, or even when the giants finally stampeded into the distance. She only knew that when she finally got her breath and tried to stand up on shaky legs, the grassland was very quiet.

"The giants are gone. We can get up now," she whispered.

"We didn't make it." Crick was already sitting. His voice was bitter. He pulled a seed pod from his tunic and hurled it to the ground far below. "Not even halfway."

"No," Ripple said bleakly. She turned to Mother, who was bending over Ivy, checking her bruises, talking to her in a low, soothing voice.

"You're *sure* you're all right, after that . . . landing?"

"Landing, my beard. It was a *crash*," Uncle growled, massaging his leg. "And *I* am not all right. My leg will never be the same. I will never be the same!" He shook his fist at the night. But his voice didn't have enough strength to sound properly angry.

"I should never have let you talk me into this." Old Ivy's eyes were angry sparks in her shadowed face. "Never. Just look where it's gotten us!"

"*They* almost got us!"

It was like a bad dream. The seven of them stranded on this high, cold giants' thing, far from the stone mountain. The night wrapped darker around them. There were fewer blinking lights now. Had the giants captured the rest of the star gods?

"Star gods," Ripple whispered to the twinkling lights, "fly back to the sky. You were safe there, star gods."

"What?" Lissa looked up in surprise. "How do you know where they came from?"

"The legend, of course." Uncle Kane's voice cut in. "You mean you don't *know* the legend? Well, then, by Nimrod, girl, you shall hear it now!"

"Now, Uncle," Mother cut in worriedly, "you should rest, get your strength back. You can tell the story later."

"Quiet!" Uncle waved Mother away irritably and took a long deep breath.

"Long ago the Mighty One made the sky and put in it the sun to warm the day and the moon and stars to light the night." Uncle's voice was still hoarse and weak, but he sat up straighter as he spoke, waving his arm toward the sky.

"The stars hung in the cold, dark sky night after night, from winter to spring to summer to fall, then to winter again. There was no change." Uncle took another deep breath. His ragged voice swelled a bit.

"On earth, the seasons changed and summer

brought with it the magic for our people, Micarus, and for the great buzzing creatures everywhere. Wings. The magic of flight. But up in the sky all was cold and still." Uncle's voice gained strength, deepened to his powerful storyteller's tone. His tiredness seemed to have vanished.

"The star gods spoke to the Mighty One, asking for a time of magic, too, so they could leave the cold sky to join the summer creatures in flight." He rolled the words out, gesturing toward the sky.

"The Mighty One granted their wish. He let the magic come to them for a brief time only. And so, each summer, some of the star gods come down from the sky and fly among us, blinking their lights through the land. Then they travel back to the sky and stay there until the next summer."

He stopped.

The story was alive, all around them: in the dark sky overhead, with its high stars, and in the yellow and green flashes of the star gods, blinking across the grassland.

And Uncle was part of the story, part of the magic, standing there on that cold giants' thing, his face glowing yellow in the pole-moonlight, and his eyes burning as if lit by their own fire.

And not just Uncle. The whole world felt changed. A silent night-land of legend and magic.

Uncle had brought the sky closer; it was a place where star gods could glide from the sky to the earth and back.

The great stone mountain did not seem so far.

And Ripple did not feel so weak.

"Diy." Crick's voice. Hushed, respectful. So he felt it too. Ripple shivered.

"We can make it," Ripple whispered. The shiver had suddenly taken hold of her whole body: an eager, excited trembling. "We *can*. We've almost crossed the whole grassland—just this one last stretch."

Old Ivy's raspy voice shook just a bit as she took hold of the cape, pulling tighter on an end knot.

"All right then—let's get it over with."

XIV

The Flight

Dark sky above, dark grass far below. They launched themselves into the night. Ripple, Pan and Lissa in front, Uncle, Crick and Mother behind.

The drag on the power was immediate. Every muscle in Ripple's body protested the extra weight this time. She worked her wings hard and fast, trying to stay aloft, to keep her balance.

"Higher," Pan yelled beside her.

Crick rose, too fast. The bag swayed, pulling Ripple off-balance.

"Careful!" she panted, beating her wings furiously to regain her balance. "We're supposed . . . to work . . . together!"

"Diy!" Crick sounded scared.

They zigzagged over the grass, wobbling and lurching like an injured bird that could not keep its balance.

Ripple's shoulders ached more each minute from the weight of the bag. Her palms burned from the rough fiber. She wanted to shut her eyes against the dizzy, sick feeling that came with each lurch. But she had to keep them open, had to keep the far-off mountain in sight, had to will her tired wings to keep moving, to fight the heavy drag, pulling them down.

Mother and Crick and Uncle pulled too hard from the back. The bag jerked, then plunged straight down.

"Fight it!" Pan yelled. "Fight!"

"Dear Nimrod, we're crashing!"

Ripple clenched her teeth, tightened her painful grip on the handle. She didn't dare glance at the cape-bag swinging so crazily below. Poor Ivy, having to depend on them, on their puny strength. It wasn't enough. They were losing height steadily now, tumbling left and right at the mercy of the air currents.

"Easy . . . easy. . . ." Mother whispered. Lissa's breaths were almost sobs; Ripple felt as if her wings would break in two under the awful strain.

They *couldn't*. The magic couldn't fail now. It had to work. She'd been so sure; they had the power.

"Special power," Uncle had said. Inside *her*.

"Magic," she whispered desperately, "magic, work for us. Magic . . . magic." She kept chanting it, grabbing onto the word itself as a lifeline.

Ma-*gic*. Ma-*gic*. She hardly realized that her wings were moving with the rhythm of the word until she heard Lissa whispering it beside her: "Ma-*gic*. Ma-*gic*."

They were saying it together now. Ma-*gic*. And their wings were working together.

Ma-*gic*. Wings-*out*. The rhythm was hypnotic.

Wings-*out*. "Ma-*gic*." Another voice joined. Crick's.

"Diy, we're doing it!"

Had the others heard it, too? The flight was

changing from the dizzy uneven swaying and bobbing to something more controlled.

"Ma-*gic!*" She was shouting it now, shouting it to the others, to the sky, the far-off mountain, to the night itself.

Ma-*gic*. That's-*it*. Wings-*out*.

We're doing it! she thought exultantly. It's working! She felt a sudden surge of power as six pairs of wings moved together in a graceful, fluid beat. And again. And again. And again—toward the stone mountain.

They might reach it. They might make it over— if they didn't lose any more height.

Close up, the stone surface was not smooth at all but harsh and forbidding.

Ma-*gic*. Ma-*gic*.

O-*ver*. O-*ver*.

The stone wall was close enough to touch.

Ma-*gic*. O-*ver*. There was panting, gasping, wheezing on all sides as they struggled higher, higher . . . o-*ver* . . . O-*ver* . . . O-*ver*. . . .

The power was a great wave pouring over them all; it was greater than the tiredness and the aches. The bag swayed beneath them; it gently bumped the top of the stone—and then they were over.

For a frozen second they hung there, triumphant: the grassland of the giants spread out on one side; on the other, a great darkness, waiting.

For that second, the magic pulsed through them like something alive; a current joining them together.

"We did it, Old Ivy," Ripple whispered to the bag. "You're over."

And then they started to drop.

Down, down, down toward the dark ground. The bag bobbing this way and that—too fast. It was like running downhill and not being able to stop. Ripple's wings beat frantically, trying to slow the momentum, to recapture the rhythm.

Are we flying or falling? she thought in panic, as the ground rushed toward them, despite her feeble wingbeats.

"Fight the drop!" There was a wild edge to Mother's voice.

It was impossible to make sense of the rushing shadows. The bag swung into a bush with a painful jerk that stopped the headlong plummet. Ripple was still blinking back tears from the sudden sharp tug on already sore hands when the rope went slack, and the bag bumped down onto the dark leafy ground.

"Are you all right, Old Ivy?"
"Here, let me help you."
They struggled in the dark to untangle the cape

ropes and open the cloak.

Old Ivy just lay there, eyes open, but without speaking or moving.

"Old Ivy, you're over the giants' mountain, truly." Lissa had almost lost her voice. The words came out in a rough croak.

Still the old woman didn't answer.

Ripple turned to Mother in alarm, her own aches and bruises forgotten. "Is she hurt?" she whispered. "Why won't she talk?" She crouched over Ivy.

"Get up. Talk," she begged. "We didn't mean to knock you into things, really." Anything—even Old Ivy's sharp-tongued comments would be better than this blank, silent stare.

Old Ivy shook her head the slightest bit: a quick angry movement. She unclenched her fist from the cape and raised her hand.

"Listen." It was a command. Hoarse and trembling.

"What?" Ripple said, puzzled. "Listen to what?"

"Shh," Pan and Mother spoke together. They stood, suddenly tense, listening.

The silence stretched out. At first Ripple heard only the many noises of the night creatures, the rustling of the wind in the leaves, and Uncle's heavy wheezing. Then, straining hard, she heard it. Not just with her ears, but with her whole body. The sound she had thought she'd never hear again. It was very faint but unmistakable.

The faraway splash of the river.

A low, wheezy voice broke the sudden hush.

"You . . . you. . . ." Uncle whispered. His eyes glowed as he stared at Ripple. "I was right. The Special Power . . . I have seen it this night."

XV

The Death-Web

It was agony, hearing that faraway call of the river and not being able to see it, not even when the sky lightened with morning.

Ripple stared at the wilderness that stretched ahead as far as she could see.

"How far away do you think it is? Do you think we're near our old colony?"

There were as many questions in her head as there were scratches and bruises on her body. She leapt up into an impatient glide, then circled back toward the others. "How far—" she began again.

"I don't know, Ripple. But if we can hear it, the river can't be too far." There was a new excitement in Mother's voice, too, this morning. No lectures about organizing and being prepared. She, too, kept staring into the distance with a soft, yearning look on her face. "Maybe we should start right out." Then she turned to Old Ivy. "That is, if you feel up to it, with that hip."

Pan looked up from the stick he was sharpening into a new spear. "We could make you a stretcher—" he began.

"Absolutely not!" Old Ivy got up, wincing a little, leaning on a stick. "This hip may be bruised a little, but I still have two perfectly good legs for walking. *And that is the only way I intend to travel from now on!*" She glared at all of them, then resolutely hobbled forward a few steps. "No sense tarrying here all morning, with the river almost within reach."

When she spoke those last words the sharpness left her voice. The fierce glare changed to another look as she stared into the forest. The edges of her mouth trembled into the smallest of smiles.

"Well, what are we waiting for?" she demanded.

"Old Ivy's right. What are we waiting for!" Crick jumped up, brandishing his newly made spear.

"No rest for the weary," Uncle groaned, rubbing his leg, pulling a prickle-weed from his ragged tunic. But it was only a halfhearted groan. He, too, was staring toward the river sounds.

He took a deep breath and stretched out his walking stick like a finger, pointing. "Such is the lot of true pioneers: to push ever onward, despite pain, fatigue, hunger"—he popped a handful of seeds into his mouth—"just as the heroes of old did, until they reached the river." His voice softened on the last two words. His eyes looked beyond them, toward the river. So Uncle felt it, too, the magical call of the river.

Ripple leapt into another quick jump-glide. "Let's *go!*" If only they could fly. It would be so easy, so fast. It took every ounce of her will power to land, to stay down on the leafy ground, to keep her wings from opening.

Did the others feel the same? Uncle was so *slow*. And as the morning wore on, Ivy had more trouble keeping up, too. Ripple knew she shouldn't feel impatient. But the longing was too great; the river calling her louder each moment.

"We *have* to reach the river soon!" She bit her lip hard. "I can't wait! I can't stand it!" She was speaking to Lissa, but Pan reached out and caught her arm.

"I know it's hard for you," he said in a low

voice. "But we can't push Uncle past his strength. Or Ivy." He pulled out a lantan weed and held it out to her, with a little wink.

"Chomp on this instead of your lips. I find it helpful."

Ripple stared at him in surprise. Pan never shared his precious lantan. Not that anyone else wanted it. Cautiously she held the weed to her mouth, then spat it out.

"Ugh! It's bitter!"

"Bitter!" Pan looked insulted. And then they were both grinning.

"That's better," Pan said with another wink.

"Pan! You're not trying to start Ripple on that filthy habit of yours!" Mother's voice was mad and teasing at the same time.

"Don't worry. The girl has no appreciation," Pan answered cheerfully, putting his arm around Mother's shoulders. "How about you?" He held a piece in front of her face, grinning that special sideways smile he kept for Mother.

"How about me?" Crick reached over and grabbed it and stuck it in his mouth.

"Great!" he declared bravely, through puckered lips. He flexed his muscles. "Gives me new energy!"

Pan gave him a playful shove. Crick grabbed Ripple, half-running, half-tumbling down the mossy hummock. "Come on. Race you!"

"Wait for me!" Lissa sprinted after them.

"Children!"

"We'll stop at the top of the next hill," Crick called back over his shoulder. "We'll wait for you there."

They clambered over roots, they jumped a small water pool, they shot into a mossy hollow, as a column of creepers marched by. They raced past a fallen twig; they jumped from a flat rock. It was just the three of them suddenly, braving the dangers of the forest, outwitting lurking enemies, conquering all. Each time Ripple crouched to hide from an enemy, she marveled again at how her wings folded down around her like a protective tent, blending with the forest colors. By keeping perfectly still, she could disappear from her enemy's sight. Wonderful magic! It not only gave her flight; it also helped to give her invisibility!

They hiked farther and the river sounds grew louder.

Ripple reached the hilltop a few seconds before Crick and Lissa. She came to an abrupt stop. Her hand went to her mouth.

"Crick! Lissa! Come here!"

There were no more hills to climb. Below her, the land sloped down for a long way. And at the bottom of the slope, barely visible between tree foliage and low brush, was water, running, splashing, sparkling in the sunlight.

The river!

"That's it! That's it!" She was jumping up and down, waving her arms, yelling. "We're almost there!"

Forgetting caution, silence, forgetting everything, she rushed down the sloping bank. Her run became a low glide.

"Wait, Ripple! We said we'd stop here!" Lissa's voice called after her. Then Crick's.

"Slow down! Diy, you're going too fast!"

Ripple heard their shouts, heard the alarm in their voices, but much more compelling was the water below. She couldn't stop. Her wings suddenly had a will of their own as she glided down the familiar clay bank, dodging the smooth river rocks.

"Stop, Ripple!" Mother's voice was loud and commanding. She had reached the top of the hill, too. Ripple turned to call back to her.

"Mother, I—"

And then she hit something. A thread wall grasped at her, tangling her in a net of horrible stickiness, catching her hair, her legs, her whole body.

A death-web. She'd rushed headlong into a

death-web! Fear pounded in her eardrums in hot painful thumps. She yanked back violently, struggling to pull free.

"Help!" she tried to scream, but the sound came out a choked whisper. "Mother! Help!" The more she fought against the strangling threads, the tighter they caught at her.

She heard Lissa scream. "Ripple's caught!"

Frantic voices, footsteps crashing down the hill.

"We'll get you free!"

"*Ripple!*" Something in Lissa's shrill cry made Ripple look up.

Great black hairy legs were moving along the edge of the web. Gigantic black legs. And above them, a shiny black evil body was coming closer, vibrating the web like a warning.

She screamed. She clawed at the threads, turning, kicking. They pulled tighter, snarling her left leg and arm completely. Stickiness trailed across her eyes, her nose, her mouth. She could hardly move her head.

The hairy legs moved closer.

"Ripple—Ripple!" Hands tugged at her from behind.

"Careful, we'll get caught, too!" Then Crick's voice changed. "Down, Lissa!"

Ripple jerked as something hurtled over her head: a dark streak of movement whizzing toward the hideous crawling black legs. The air hummed with its speed. There was a cry somewhere behind her. Then another dark streak whistling overhead, sinking into the shiny black body.

"Got it!" She heard shouts, footsteps, more voices. Hands pulled at her, untangling her from the terrifying web.

"Easy, easy; we'll get you out." Someone was hacking away the snarled stickiness; someone else was dragging her back, onto the moss.

She lay there, shaking all over.

"Ripple. Oh, Ripple!" Mother was crying, pulling at the thread strands that still stuck to Ripple's hair. "Won't you *ever* learn?"

"But who threw that second spear?"

More footsteps. A sudden confusion of voices crying out, interrupting one another.

"By all the gods and pioneers!" Uncle's voice rang out above the others.

"No. I don't believe it." Mother's arm went slack around Ripple.

What was going on? Ripple struggled to her elbows, still trembling. She rubbed her eyes, blinked, then blinked again.

Was she dreaming? That bearded face . . . wonderfully familiar . . . coming toward her.

"Ripple, remember me? Lark? I was scouting this part of the riverbank when I heard you scream."

She stared. Lark. A scout. From her colony.

"That was a mighty close call you just had."

"But . . . but. . . ." She was shaking too hard

to talk. Her teeth chattered.

Tanned arms went around her in a hard, strong hug. And then came the wonderful impossible words, flowing like smooth water over the jumble in her dizzy head, blocking out all the other excited voices around her.

"The new cove is not far. I can take you there."

XVI

The River

"After the giants' invasion, we moved downriver," Lark said. "No giants have found us—yet."

"I can't believe we're back," Mother said for the fifth time. "You—the colony—the river." She shook her head. "I just . . . can't believe it."

"Finding *you* is unbelievable." Lark's gaze swept their group, resting curiously on the strangers, Crick, Lissa, Pan, and Old Ivy. Then he turned to Mother. "After the invasion of the giants, we gave up hope of ever seeing you or Uncle Kane or Ripple again. The giants—"

"Ah, yes . . . the giants!" Uncle cut in loudly. "Young man, *we* can tell you a thing or two about giants. You are looking at ones who have stared the beasts in the *face* and lived to tell of it. In the *face*." Uncle seemed to grow taller as he spoke.

"And we've just crossed through the forbidden lands!" Crick boasted, hoisting his spear.

"Unbelievable." Lark shook his head. Then he pulled a weed from his pouch and chewed on it, letting the end dangle from the corner of his mouth.

Ripple glanced at Crick, then Lissa. They all burst out laughing.

"Not another lantan chewer!" Mother rolled her eyes, grinning.

Lark looked confused. "It's not lantan. It's rushweed."

"Doesn't matter," Mother said, looking at Pan with a twinkle in her eye. "One filthy weed's the same as another."

Pan had been standing very straight, almost wary, as Lark talked with Mother and Uncle. Now he reached down and plucked his own weed from the ground. A browner weed than Lark's. Lantan. He stuck it in his mouth and looked at Lark. Then slowly, almost reluctantly, he grinned.

"See, Pan, you'll feel right at home here!" Crick clapped him on the shoulder. Then, to Ripple's astonishment, Mother pulled the lantan out of Pan's mouth and kissed him.

Crick whistled.

The happiness was too much. Ripple couldn't wait a second more. Eagerness and energy had replaced the numb shock from the death-web.

"Come on! Let's go down to the water!" She started down the final stretch of bank.

"This time watch where you're going!" her mother called.

As if she could stop watching! Her eyes darted everywhere, taking it all in, hungrily: the gleaming river rocks, the soft, mossy logs, the churning water, splashing up to meet her like an old friend.

Then she stopped in surprise.

She was not the first one to reach the river. Old Ivy stood ankle-deep in the water, staring out over its sparkling blueness.

When had she left the group? Ripple hadn't even seen her go.

"Old Ivy—" she said softly.

Quickly Ivy leaned over and splashed water on her face. She turned to Ripple. The water drops ran like small rivers down her cheeks. A funny feeling pulled at Ripple's stomach. That wetness wasn't all from the river. There was a glittery brightness in the old woman's eyes.

"Well, so you made it back," was all Old Ivy said.

"So did you," Ripple answered. For a second the two of them stood there, staring at each other.

She feels it, too, Ripple thought in surprise. Of all the people in the group, it's Old Ivy who feels it the most, the pull of the river.

The next moment Crick skidded beside them with a whoop.

"Diy, such a lot of water!" He leaned on his spear. "Diy," he said again, his eyes wide with wonder.

"It *is* like a live creature," Lissa said softly, dropping beside Ripple. She dipped her fingers in the running water. "Just like you told us, Ripple. No—it's even better!"

"We go west to reach the new cove." Lark joined them. "It's not too far—" He paused, staring around the group with a little smile. "I get the feeling no one is listening."

They were all still staring at the river.

"From the giants' bottle prison, to the new forest, across the dangerous forbidden lands—to this." Uncle drew in a long, deep breath, as if he were trying to inhale the whole flavor, the moment. "Such a tale we shall have for them!"

Lissa spoke:

"When the pioneers reached the Land of the Giants, they faced new dangers. Giants threw great round, red weapons at them. They tried to stomp them into the ground with their great feet. They hurled them into the sky. They chased them with evil bottles to try and recapture them." Lissa's voice was a fierce, low whisper. "But they could not catch the pioneers. The pioneers made it across the great grassland, and over the high mountain— and returned to the land of their people." She glanced at Ripple. "They crossed with the power of the magic. Special Power came to them that night. And so—they reached the river."

No one broke the silence until Lark laid an arm gently on Uncle's shoulder. He beckoned to the rest of them.

"The new cove is this way. Come with me."

XVII

Home

The trail was narrow, well-hidden by riverbank weeds that had to be pushed aside, and rocks that had to be climbed or walked around. But Ripple hardly noticed the weeds, hardly saw the rocks, until she tripped over them, hardly heard Uncle's voice boasting: "I tell you, we have been snatched from the jaws of death." Then, in a lower voice, to Ivy: "The elders of the colony will remember you. See if they don't."

"Poppy-rot," Ivy snorted. "It's been too long."

The words swirled around Ripple without sinking in. Her eyes, her ears, her whole body was tuned to the water, flowing beside them along the trail and now starting to glow pink with the evening sky. Her wonderful river that she thought she'd never see again.

Rip-ple. Rip-ple. It was calling her.

The magic trembled through her like a creature

struggling to break free.

Rip-ple. Rip-ple.

She hardly noticed the ground dropping away below her. She was above the water, the foam splashing at her playfully while she skimmed above the wavelets. She dipped and soared, circling higher, higher.

"Ripple!" Mother's voice called out, "You'll get lost! You'll lose the trail!"

"Oh, she'll be all right." Old Ivy's voice was firm. "Let her fly."

Ripple looked down. Her eyes met Old Ivy's across the water. In that split second, Ripple suddenly saw past the wrinkles and the hump, saw the long-ago girl who loved to fly, to explore, an adventurous girl—who went too far.

We're alike, Old Ivy and I, she thought with a little tingle of surprise. Old Ivy, who had no wings, knew. This was what wings were for. This was the real power and freedom of the magic—to soar over the river.

And yet the magic had changed even that old friend. From this height, she could see the curving banks of the river, leading to far-off places.

The river wasn't the whole world. She knew that now. She flew higher. The sunset pink deepened to red. Fiery red, burning the sky above, the water below, touching her wings with fire-color.

Higher . . . higher. She could feel the power, the strength swelling inside her. She could reach the top of the sky! Exhilarating, frightening—the power of the magic inside her. Was it the "special magic"?

Crick and Lissa flew up toward her. Their faces, their hair, their tunics glowed red-gold.

"Ripple, hurry!" Lissa cried. "We've reached the cove!"

"Where is it?" Ripple's heart skipped a beat.

"Down there. See it?" Crick pointed at the bank. Then he flipped into one of his daredevil dives, swooping straight for the bank. Lissa followed.

"Come on, Ripple!"

"Where?" Ripple yelled again, straining to see in the red glare.

There was a sheltered inlet, protected by a large, overhanging tree. The tree's leaves hid the inside of the cove from view, but there, on the rock jutting over the water—people! Lots of people!

She flew faster.

Loud excited voices floated up to her.

" . . . come back!"

"Kane! Fern!"

"But—who are these!"

Ripple's heart thudded crazily, painfully. Her eyes stung with a sudden wetness that turned the scene below to a red blur. Those voices . . . *her* people. . . .

"We shall need a Gathering!" Uncle's voice rose above the others, loud and important.

And then a younger voice broke through the noise.

"Look! It's Ripple!" A girl was pointing up toward the sky. Ripple knew that girl. Rusha.

"I'm coming!" she yelled.

They were all watching her now.

" . . . come back. From the Giants," a shrill voice cried.

The words hung below her in the red-gold sky like the first whispers of a legend.